CACTUS - DREAMS

By

Frank C. Senia

All Rights Reserved.

No part of this book may be used or reproduced by any means, graphic, electronic, or mechanical, including photocopying, or by any information storage retrieval system without the written permission of the owner except with brief quotations in articles and reviews.

This book is a work of fiction. Unless otherwise shown, the names, characters, businesses, places, events, and incidents are products of the author's imagination or used fictitiously. Any resemblance to actual persons, living or dead, or events is coincidental.

Copyright © 2024 by Frank C. Senia

TABLE OF CONTENTS

CHAPTER-1 4

CHAPTER 3 24

CHAPTER 4 34

CHAPTER 5 45

CHAPTER 6 58

CHATER 7 74

CHAPTER 8 90

CHAPTER 9 102

CHAPTER 10 115

CHAPTER 10 127

CHAPTER 11 136

CHAPTER 12 147

CHAPTER 13 157

CHAPTER 14 169

CHAPTER 15 182

CHAPTER-1

Imagine, if you will, a place in the Mexican desert, where the sun blazes like an unyielding fire, and in this very place, a young boy named Antonio calls home. His home, a modest adobe house, had endured years of scorching summers that left its walls baked.

Antonio's days were filled with the secrets of the vast desert, where he would immerse himself in the enchanting whispers of the wind, marvel at the towering saguaros that have stood for centuries, and unravel the hidden mysteries that lay beneath the sandy dunes. Antonio had the remarkable ability to transport himself to different places through his vivid imagination, which served as an escape from the harshness of reality.

Despite facing numerous challenges and setbacks, he never wavered in his determination to immigrate to America and fulfill his entrepreneurial dream of owning a Bar and Grill.

In his dreams, he envisioned a future where he would assert his individuality and had meticulously outlined all the specifics. By achieving his desire, Antonio would not only make his father proud but also acquire the ability to support his family. Why a Bar and Grill?

When Antonio reflects on his childhood memories, one thing that stands out vividly is his grandfather Alfredo's bustling life as the owner and operator of a charming cafe. This cafe had a delightful patio, with tables strategically placed to create the perfect ambiance. The tables and chairs at this venue are not only large and round, but they are also made of beautiful red wood. Additionally, each table is accompanied by a tall umbrella, featuring a striking red and white plaid color scheme.

Antonio has fond memories of being at the restaurant as a child, where he would run from table to table engaging in conversations with customers. Additionally, he continues to dedicate his weekends and after-school hours to assisting his grandfather. When the customers left, they expressed their appreciation for his service by leaving a tip on the tables, which served as his compensation. This gave him the opportunity to not only financially help support his parents but also enjoy the luxury of having additional funds in his pockets.

The image of grandpa sitting with others, playing cards and enjoying a beer, was etched into his mind. He has held onto this fantasy for a countless number of years.

Antonio's father Juan, was a weathered cowboy who worked on a ranch, caring for horses and cleaning the barn. His father's eyes reminiscent of breathtaking sunsets, imparted upon him the invaluable skill of reading the land. Antonio's father would take him riding the horses boarded in the barn.

Riding their horses across the arid expanse, their hooves created dust storms and together they formed a mesmerizing scene.

Antonio dedicated himself to developing the skill of interpreting the hidden messages conveyed by the rustling mesquite leaves, which allowed him to hone his ability to listen keenly. Possessing a remarkable intuition, he had the extraordinary ability to anticipate the imminent arrival of rain, detecting its approach well in advance, sometimes even before the initial distant rumble of thunder could be heard.

Among the various plants he encountered, it was the saguaro cacti that held the greatest fascination for him. Like the guardians of old, they assumed a timeless posture, their arms reaching upwards as if to touch the heavens above. Antonio's father took the time to explain to his son that every cactus had a fascinating story behind it, with each tale meticulously etched into their spines.

The cacti appeared to have a mystical connection with history, as if they had observed firsthand the encounters between Apache warriors, Spanish conquistadors, and gold-seeking prospectors. Delving into the captivating world of the cactus, he would meticulously study its historical significance, drawing inspiration from its intriguing past.

While the sun was blazing overhead and turning the desert into a fiery canvas of orange and crimson, Antonio's fortuitous discovery led him to stumble upon a secret oasis. Amid the vibrant red rocks, there is a tranquil pool of refreshing water, its surface shimmering like a mirage in the vast desert.

It was in that very location that he came face to face with Luna, a girl whose eyes were strikingly reminiscent of the captivating shade of turquoise. He questioned whether she was a real person or a figment of his imagination, particularly because of the significance of her presence.

With a graceful emergence from the water, her long locks cascaded down her shoulders, resembling delicate strands of shimmering silver. Was this the girl of his dreams? Being just fifteen, they both locked eyes.

Antonio entertained the thought that Luna's declaration of being a desert spirit, an overseer of abandoned reveries, could be purely a manufacture of his imagination. With a tribal brown dress gracefully draped around her, water cascading down its sides, she approached him and took a seat next to him by the pond. It was at that point that she began her speech. Asking his name.

She spoke of ancient rituals and whispered promises. He listened, entranced by her otherworldly tales. She told him that the saguaros held the key to unlocking hidden dominions: their spines were portals to places beyond imagination.

His curiosity grew. He began to visit the saguaros at night, when the moon bathed the desert in silver. With Luna's guidance, he pressed his palms against their rough skin and thorns, feeling the pulse of energy. And then, one fateful night, a cactus split open like a secret door. The ethereal essence of António gracefully passed through, severing ties with the physical world and leaving the ground behind.

The moment he stepped into the twilight desert, he was mesmerized by the celestial spectacle of stars shimmering and moving about like fireflies. The giant saguaros, with their towering heights, reached out towards the enchanting violet sky, and their branches were adorned with countless constellations. Luna made her appearance, and as she did, she took him by the hand and guided him further into this enchanting and mystical world, where the passage of time seemed to be altered, and where dreams materialized before their very eyes.

Antonio discovered he could communicate with the spirits of the desert. They whispered forgotten stories—the love of a lost cowboy, the courage of a Native warrior, and the sorrow of a lonely miner. Each saguaro held fragments of these lives, awaiting someone to listen.

As the summer gradually ended, Antonio found himself assuming the role of a bridge connecting different domains. Positioned beneath the saguaros, he would sit cross-legged, fully engrossed in the important task of translating their secrets from the wind. Positioned in front of him, he watches Luna, while the sound of laughter reverberates through the canyons. By joining forces, they skillfully crafted a tapestry of memories that breathed life into the desert, leaving an enduring mark on its surface.

But with every gift comes a price. c felt the weight of time pulling at his bones. He aged faster, his hair growing like the sagebrush.

Luna soon grew distant, fading into starlight. She told him that he had a choice, to remain in the desert as a keeper of stories, or return to the mortal world.

With one last glance at the twilight desert, he bravely stepped back through the cactus portal, ready to embrace whatever awaited him on the other side. However, deep inside him, he held the enchantment of the desert, with its secrets whispered by the saguaros, the ethereal flavor of stardust, and the unforgettable image of Luna's mesmerizing turquoise eyes.

And so, in the Arizona desert, António became a storyteller. His tales echoed the ancient saguaros, infusing them with the dreams of forgotten souls. He had an endless supply of stories that seemed to flow effortlessly from deep within his soul, captivating the ears of everyone who listened. His words flowed like desert rivers, carving canyons of wonder. A boy who never wrote before now has the ability to describe successful and wonderful moments.

If you ever visit the scorched expanse, listen closely. You might hear Antonio's voice in the wind, weaving tales of cactus dreams and the girl who danced among the stars, Luna.

In the depths of his mind, Luna has assumed the significant role of his spirit guardian, acting as a courier and embodying his life force.

Just before disappearing into the twinkling starlit heavens, she informed Antonio that whenever he required assistance or guidance, all he had to do was shut his eyes and conjure up her appearance, complete with her captivating face and intense, penetrating emerald eyes. Only when that special moment arrived would she reveal herself to him, penetrating his mind and soul, becoming the source of his inspiration.

CHAPTER 2

As Antonio reaches the mature age of sixteen, he realized he had no future in the small town of Oaxaca, Mexico but only to wind up like his father - a work hand on a horse farm. With an unwavering determination to achieve his lifelong dream, he made the courageous decision to gather all of his belongings, meticulously pack them up, and use every single penny he had diligently saved over the years, just so he could embark on his journey to America. Despite his fear and confusion, he realized that now was the perfect moment to seek guidance from Luna.

As he made his way out the front door of his home, he embarked on a journey into the dark desert night, driven by the desire to find the tranquil pool of water hidden among the majestic red rock formations. Mesmerized by the sight of the moon's glow reflecting on the pond in the distance, he instinctively made his way towards it, with the sole purpose of locating a towering saguaro cactus that would allow him to conjure up the vision of Luna. As he searched for his ideal location, he sat in a crossed-legged position, with his head held down, his big brown eyes closed, and began to think about the vision of Luna, his spirit guardian.

The more time passed, the more he longed for her appearance, his impatience growing with every passing moment. From the depths of the pitch-black sky, a sudden, and powerful bolt of lightning illuminated the surroundings, directly hitting the cactus that stood before him. The impact made a terrifying sound that sent shivers down Antonio's spine.

As he opens his eyes, he is met with the stunning sight of giant saguaro cacti that appear to be split in two, as if they were the gates of heaven unveiling before him. Luna gracefully emerged from the center of the towering plant in a serene and gentle manner, extending her hand toward him and inviting him to approach her. António bravely moves ahead, taking a step forward and confidently entering through the open saguaro door to be with Luna. Luna and António took a seat on the deep red soil, their bodies sinking into its softness. Luna, with her mesmerizing emerald eyes locked onto him, poses a question to António, asking how she can offer him her unwavering support.

In a burst of impatience, he enthusiastically informs her about his intentions to depart from Oaxaca, Mexico, and begin his voyage to the United States. Luna, with a calm and serene demeanor, finds herself deep in thought, as a multitude of opinions pass through her mind, while she ponders and meditates on the important decision ahead.

While maintaining eye contact with Antonio, Luna's gentle voice resonates as she affirms, "As I peer into the depths of your eyes, I am able to sense with utmost certainty in both my heart and spirit that the forthcoming decision is the correct path to choose."

She rises, takes Antonio's hand, and leads him back outside the depths of the inner cactus. Showing her love and care, she leans down to kiss his head and wishes him a safe journey with her blessing. It has become evident to him that he is making the right decision.

In a quick and agile manner, he makes his way back to his home, leaving behind a swirling cloud of dust as evidence of his haste. Upon entering his modestly sized room, he proceeds to open his closet in search of several essential belongings that he plans to bring along, placing them on his sleeping cot.

While rummaging through his closet, he discovered an old wood box in the dusty corners of his closet with an ancient-looking etching on it. Brushing away the cobwebs and dust, his curiosity piqued.

Wondering what he had discovered, his excitement drew him to open the old box as a smile spread across his face. Upon opening the box, he found an old map, drawn on aged parchment paper. That evening, he spent hours engrossed in the map, pouring over it with successful concentration, leaving no detail unnoticed. His efforts paid off when he discovered the map presented a path that would guide him across the majestic Reo Grand River, eventually leading to a specific spot marked by an enigmatic X. The query that lingered in his thoughts was: Where does this captivating map ultimately lead to?

Now, he was determined more than ever to make his journey to America and discover what treasure this map may lead him to. Several days later, while in town, amidst the oppressive heat and merciless sun of the Sonoran Desert, he reached out to a local coyote named Carlos for help navigating the intricate network of hidden paths and the seemingly endless expanse of barren sand, all in pursuit of crossing the U.S. border.

With a muted gesture, he decided to leave a note on the kitchen table before he departed, intending for his parents to read it and understand his actions, particularly as they were asleep at the moment.

Antonio found himself sitting at a table that was faintly lit, positioned next to an open window that allowed the gentle, warm wind to seep inside and speak to him. Guided by the whispers of the wind, he felt compelled to openly declare his love for his mother, who diligently toiled as a dedicated worker at the horse farm.

His profound love for his parents is one of the deciding factors driving him to embark on an adventurous journey that will bring positive changes to all their lives in the future.

The act of writing the memo brought forth a flood of emotions, causing tears to cascade down his face. The words flowed effortlessly from his mind, making their way down to the tip of the pen. It is a fact that he will deeply miss both of them, and it is anticipated that upon reading his note, they will experience immense pain. However, he is driven with a deep commitment to make this journey.

Returning to his room, he gathered his backpack, walked to the door, and then turned to look back at his home, where he had spent the last sixteen years. Each item brought back a childhood memory. With feelings of sorrow, he walks out of his house, contemplating the possibility that it may be his last time doing so.

Later that evening, in the moonless night, with stars winking above, Antonio and a group of fellow travelers embarked on the same journey, following a wiry man named Carlos, who possessed an intimate knowledge of the trails, as if they were etched on the lines of his palms.

With utmost caution, the group skillfully maneuvered, ensuring they went unnoticed by the ever-vigilant border patrol.

Upon reaching the border, their destination - the United States, a land filled with hope - they faced the daunting task of crossing the Rio Grande River, its murky waters and strong current posing a challenge as it tugged at their legs. Carlos's persistent yelling of "Keep moving!" served as a constant reminder to everyone to not stop and to keep progressing. "Hesitation is something we cannot afford as we are pressed for time," he added.

António's heart pounded with a mix of fear and excitement as he embarked on this journey, which was completely new to him. Upon reaching the land on the other side of the river in America, he carefully retrieved his map, which had been securely wrapped in plastic, to secure it from any water damage, and to his relief, it had successfully endured the journey. As the entourage continued on its way, Antonio decided to separate himself from the group.

In his search, he was seeking a location that was both mute and serene. Once he stumbled upon it, he chose a spot beside a majestic saguaro cactus and comfortably crossed his legs. After reaching that point, he followed the precise instructions Luna had provided him with and proceeded to call upon her. The night sky was enveloped in darkness, with thick clouds covering the entire expanse and obscuring any glimpse of stars in the heavens.

With confidence in Luna's ability to answer, he sat patiently, his heart pounding in anticipation, eagerly awaiting her response. Then it happened, a flash of light striking the saguaro near him, opening a gateway to its soul. Luna appeared before him and asked him what he needed. He shared with her the exciting news of his recent discovery, a map that he had stumbled upon, and his ambitious plan to embark on a journey following its markings.

Luna encouraged him to pursue his dreams, as there may be a treasure awaiting him or there may not be. Her advice to Antonio is to rely on his instincts moving forward, with the reassurance that she will be available to support him in times of great urgency. While she retreats into the prickly cactus, Antonio, feeling utterly exhausted from his extensive travels, eventually succumbs to fatigue and drifts into a deep sleep.

As Antonio awakens, he is momentarily blinded by the brilliance of the sun rising over the mountain. As his eyes gradually adapt to the surroundings, he realizes he is located in the midst of nowhere, with nothing but endless stretches of sand dunes and desert vegetation encompassing his vision. In the midst of his voyage, a sense of solitude washes over him, prompting him to quench his thirst with multiple swallows of water from his canteen.

As he moved into a shaded area filled with rocks, he decided to take out his map to locate his current position. With caution, he removed his trusted compass from his backpack and proceeded to study the directions in front of him.

His compass pointed north, the direction he wanted to travel. The map showed a trail along the Rio Grande River crossing between two pinnacle mountain peaks. In the distance, he could see the two mountain peaks. Are they the ones drawn on the map? His instinct tells him to walk in that direction.

The map shows a pyramid-like structure between the mountains. Could it be a temple or an ancient structure? Could that location be the mysterious place? With his eyes widening and heart pounding, he quickens his pace forward. He feels he is getting close to the X-marked spot.

With each step he took, the ancient structure became more visible and defined. The intricate carvings and the mysterious weather gave the impression that this place might contain hidden secrets. The scorching morning sun has left Antonio feeling parched, famished, and drenched in sweat. He is standing just a few yards away from the small ancient structure, which bears a striking resemblance to a burial crypt rather than a temple.

A wood door, notable for its size and weight, can be found at the front entrance. Leaning against the old door, he sits on the ground and contemplates the various ways he can open it. Antonio, feeling thirsty, extended his arm towards his canteen and proceeded to gulp down the last few drops of water it contained.

With its composition of old, dry wood, the door presents a formidable obstacle that will require successful effort to break open. In a sudden turn of events, a small swirling gust of wind unexpectedly makes its way towards Antonio. Reacting swiftly, Antonio instinctively moves away from the door as the sand starts swirling in front of it. Surprisingly, as if by some enchantment, the door mystifyingly opens. Was Luna, watching over him, helping him succeed in his adventure?

CHAPTER 3

Carefully, he stepped inside, his footsteps echoing in the hollow space. The interior is faintly lit, just the rays of light from the open door, let in shafts of sunlight. As he observes the cumbering walls of clay and dirt, he sees nothing but an empty shell.

As the sunlight casts its glow, it illuminates a mural that appears to portray a captivating scene from the distant past, depicting an ancient civilization that existed numerous years ago. Upon closer inspection, one can observe that the walls are covered in mysterious etchings and markings. But, what did they say or mean?

Do you think maybe the map holds valuable information that may provide insights into the meaning of these mysterious drawings? Do you think these are clues that can be solved like a puzzle? Antonio's mind spins with numerous possibilities.

With great curiosity, he takes the map out of his pocket and closely inspects it, only to discover a marking at the bottom that bears a strong resemblance to the etching found on the wall. Could it be a clue?

As he delved deeper into the challenge of deciphering the markings on the map, time seemed to slip away unnoticed, as daylight dissipated. Antonio could feel the sweat beading on his brow, but refused to quit. The task at hand involves carefully inspecting every single drawing and etching that adorns the four walls of the room.

Thirsty and hungry, his stomach sings for food. Spending most of his life in the desert, he searches for a Prickly pear cactus, which offers a delightful culinary adventure and the moisture needed for nutrition. Seeking the bright green firm pads of the Prickly pear, he stumbles upon a cactus green, lush, containing young pads. The memory that remains etched in his mind is that of his mom carefully picking the pads and relishing their succulent and delightful taste. Taking out his trusty pocket knife, he skillfully removes the peel from multiple pieces of fruit, deftly slicing them in half, and then eagerly indulging in the juicy flesh. Antonio knows the cuisine of the cactus is nutritious and he savors the flavor. His hunger is gone now.

As the sun sets and the room becomes dark, Antonio remains dedicated to staying until he uncovers what the map is hiding. With the front door removed from the cabin, he builds a small fire near the doorway using his flint. Intending to keep himself comfortable and safe during the chilly desert night, he will ensure he has the necessary warmth and visibility to continue his search of the old adobe.

While observing the flickering flames from the fire, he suddenly discovers an etching that bears a striking resemblance to the symbol depicted on his map. This newfound information causes him to reflect on the possibility that there may be a link between the two. Slowly, he inches his way toward the wall, carefully examining the map's image and comparing it to the symbol on the wall. To his surprise, he discovers they are an exact match, identical in every detail.

By taking a rock and forcefully striking it against the clay wall, the surface crumbles, resulting in the creation of an open portal within the wall. Antonio reaches into the unknown, his curiosity piqued, unsure of what he will discover. To his surprise, his hand touches a cloth bag filled with metal coins. Intrigued, he carefully removes the sack and places it on the floor, taking out a knife to cut it open. As he does so, he pours the contents onto the floor, and his amazement grows as he realizes he has found twenty-one-ounce gold coins.

Luna's wise advice to embark on the journey proved to be correct, as he ultimately found his fortune. Given today's prices, the treasure's value, based on the gold it contains, could be around $50,000 U.S. dollars. His chest swells with pride, and his spirits and hopes escalate, and he is in ecstasy.

In the late hours of the evening, around midnight, a dazzling flash of light suddenly emerges from the doorway, conjuring the apparition of Luna right in front of Antonio. As their eyes meet, a powerful connection is established, and he finds himself irresistibly drawn into the depths of her captivating emerald eyes and soul. In that moment, he feels a profound sense of happiness and gratitude for the decision he made to embark on this life-changing journey. Luna, tells him, "Antonio, seize this opportunity now to embark on a path that will allow you to pursue your passions and turn your dreams into reality. I have to attend to others who are dependent on my guidance and watchful eye."

    Luna, with grace and elegance, disports into the embrace of the dark starry night and swiftly vanishes like a fleeting bolt of lightning, ascending into the vast heavens above.

    The following morning, António gathers his belongings, places the bag of gold in his backpack, and continues his walk north, to the nearest major city, Tucson. Amidst the stillness and sweltering temperatures of the desert, he embarked on a walk, allowing himself to be captivated by the whispers of the wind, which conveyed profound messages to him. They assure him his journey will be safe and rewarding.

As he was walking along the old dirt back road, he unexpectedly discovered an old hermit farmer who was living in a neglected and deteriorating home. He approached the porch and knocked on the door several times.

When the door opened before him stood an old man perhaps eighty years of age, wearing dirty old jeans and a torn tee shirt. His face weathered by years of desert sun, a long gray beard, and teeth missing. His voice was soft and weak. The first words he spoke, "What the hell do you want kid?"

In a timid and shy manner, António approached the man and inquired if he could kindly provide him with some water and perhaps some additional food. Upon being invited, he graciously received a bottle of water and a dish of beans, served in a dish that originated from a can on a wall shelf. Antonio welcomes the charity. With great enthusiasm, he eagerly drank the water and devoured the beans like a famished dog who hadn't eaten in days.

Asking the old man's name, the reply was simply, "Rusty."

Antonio recounts his adventurous journey from Mexico, specifically aimed towards reaching Tucson, to Rusty. According to Rusty, Antonio still have a long walk ahead of him, approximately another two hundred miles.

Knowing he cannot walk that distance in the scorching desert sun, he removes a gold coin, offering it to Rusty who had an old pickup truck parked in front of his house. Antonio said, " I will give you this coin, worth $ 2,000 if you drive me to Tucson."

Rusty, eyes wide open like a tiger spotting its prey, replies, " When do you want to leave kid?"

António said, "How about now, Rusty."

Rusty tells him, he will be ready in ten minutes, he has to pee first and grab several bottles of water for the ride which will take about four hours.

Antonio goes out of the house and settles himself into the worn-out truck. The floor of the vehicle is scattered with a variety of empty beer and whiskey bottles, serving as a reminder of countless late nights and conversations that Rusty must have had that faded into oblivion. Amongst the sea of discarded bottles, there is a layer of trash and cigarette butts, evidence of a life consumed by vices and disregard for cleanliness.

All Antonio was concerned about was getting a ride to Tucson. Rusty, enters the truck holding two bottles of water, starts the engine, and off the go. As he settled into the cozy passenger seat, the jolting and uneven ride started to make him feel drowsy. As his eyes grew heavy, he could not help but see vivid visions of his beloved hometown of Oaxaca, Mexico, swirling in his mind.

The lingering scent of mezcal and marigolds was deeply ingrained in his memory. The melodic tunes of mariachi bands filled the night sky, creating an enchanting atmosphere as if they were performing a special serenade exclusively for the moon.

As the wind blew, he could distinctly hear the echoes of the old west passing through Tombstone, with gunfights resonating along the dusty dirt roads. The winds whispered enchanting tales to him, stories of daring gamblers, graceful dancers, and the ghostly presence of legends such as Wyatt Earp and Doc Holliday, all forever engraved in the tapestry of time.

When he opened his eyes, he was greeted with the sight of the bustling city of Tucson, its many new and sparkling buildings stretching out before him in the distance. It finally occurred to him that he was within a short distance of only ten miles. While getting closer to the city, an awe-inspiring symphony of saguaro cacti suddenly emerged.

He knew he could connect with Luna at any moment by gazing at the breathtaking sight of this magnificent cactus. Approaching the outskirts of the city, Antonio asked Rusty to drop him off in the poor rundown area of Tucson.

Rusty reveals to him the hidden and overlooked areas of Tucson, which are filled with struggling residents and abandoned development. One such neighborhood, called San Ignacio Yaqui, is located in the heart of Tucson and has been forgotten for a long time. In this neighborhood, the aroma of tortillas and chili lingers, creating a unique atmosphere.

Antonio requested he be dropped off there. Upon the truck coming to a stop, Rusty expresses his appreciation for the generous payment, warmly shakes Antonio's hand, and then proceeds to drive off toward his home.

CHAPTER 4

Given the intricate nature of the challenge, transforming a gold coin into U.S. dollars would undoubtedly require significant effort and be considered quite arduous. After walking the streets for quite some time, Antonio eventually stumbles upon a pawn shop. Upon entering the shop, the walls were adorned with an impressive collection of guitars and an assortment of seemingly useless artifacts, the owner of the establishment, Oscar, warmly greets him. The store, with its timeless presence, gave the impression that it had been established since the dawn of civilization. "How can I help you, son?" Oscar asked.

Antonio produces a gold coin knowing the value is worth at least $2000. Oscar asked, "What do you want to do with this gold coin?" António replied, "Turn it into U.S. dollars."

After removing his eye loop to get a better view of the coin, Oscar states he will pay $1,000 U.S. for it. António responds, "That amount is only half of its actual worth."

Oscar, with a solemn expression on his face, vigorously shakes his head while tightly clutching his mouth shut, as if trying to suppress his emotions. He said, "This is the amount of cash I have at the moment, kid. So, would you like to have it or not?"

Despite his hesitation, Antonio reluctantly agrees to the transaction and proceeds to stuff his pockets with ten one-hundred-dollar bills.

As he walked toward the door, he noticed a bulletin board with a sign saying, "Room for Rent."

Upon asking about the room for lease, Antonio returns to Oscar and inquires about obtaining more details. Oscar informs him that the room available for accommodation is located at his residence, where his wife has a vacant guest room. They have been considering the need to supplement their income because of the slow business in the porn shop industry.

Oscar informs Antonio that the rent for the apartment is $500 dollars per month and he also mentions that it is furnished. In addition, you will have the added benefit of having access to the kitchen and your own personal bathroom.

Sight unseen, Antonio blurts out, "I will take it."

Seeing how desperate Antonio is, Oscar starts feeling guilty for only giving him half the value of the coins, so he offers Antonio the first month's rent for free. And so a friendship is formed.

Oscar shuts down the shop and he kindly accompanies Antonio on a short walk, guiding him several blocks until they reach his home. Entering with Oscar, he meets his wife, Mary. Both were in their sixties, with gray hair, overweight, and looking much older. Despite this, it is evident that they come across as pleasant and trustworthy individuals.

The house is an old 1950s adobe two-bedroom, two-bath home, decorated in old-fashioned Spanish style with dark wood antique furniture. Certainly, an enormous step up from his home in Mexico.

Antonio's face lights up with delight and awe as he watches Mary open the door to the guest room. With his new living arrangement, he can now enjoy the comfort of a double bed, adorned with a red floral area carpet. The placement of the bed on a stunning wood floor elevates the overall aesthetic of the room. Furthermore, the inclusion of a small desk and a television surpasses anything he has ever possessed. Both Oscar and Mary closed the door and left the room to allow Antonio to settle in.

Antonio, taking care not to disturb the cleanliness of the bed, gently places his backpack on it. Following that, he proceeds to remove his soiled clothing carefully before making his way into the bathroom, where he turns on the shower to begin his cleansing ritual. He has not had a bath in days, and the Reo Grand River is definitely not a suitable substitute.

As the night approaches, he opens the one window in the room, enjoying the stillness that surrounds him and listening intently to the warm wind as it whispers messages to him. The wind, with its gentle whispers, carries the stories of the numerous years Oscar and Mary have spent living in this home, and tells him of a time when their son used to occupy this very room. The wind whispers about the tragic event that took Mary and Oscar's son away in an auto accident when he was a teen.

Antonio, with his special gift, can envision the shocking moment of this event. The wind whispers the story in detail to him as he lies in bed peaceably. As he thought to himself, he realized he would need to gather more information about their son.

Despite the lingering exhaustion from his travels, he manages to find solace in the peaceful embrace of sleep, as the gentle wind softly sings him a lullaby.

As the sun begins to rise, he wakes up early and is greeted by the strong, abrupt rays of sunlight, shining directly into his eyes. With a sense of disbelief, he scans the room, taking in his surroundings for a moment. This room is his. In complete silence, he cautiously opens the door and proceeds to quietly navigate through the house, taking care not to disturb Oscar and Mary who are deep in slumber.

Quietly approaching the back patio door, he gently opens it and makes his way outside to the patio. As he observed the yard, his attention was drawn to a magnificent sight - a large saguaro cactus with three arms, standing tall at approximately fifteen feet. It was both surprising and fascinating to discover that this cactus, which was positioned in the yard's corner, could be over a hundred years old. With each step he took, feeling the soft sand beneath his bare feet, he drew nearer to the massive saguaro. Eventually, he abruptly stopped walking, and a specific thought suddenly dawned on him.

"This is the spot where Luna can be summoned by me."

Once he returns to the interior of the house, he takes a seat at the kitchen table and begins to observe the various appliances it houses. Among the numerous appliances in the kitchen are a dishwasher, an oven, a toaster, and various other items. Overwhelmed by the magnitude of the blessing, he finds it hard to believe what has happened to him. While he was deep in meditation, Mary suddenly entered the room and uttered the following words, "Antonio, it seems like you are up early today, is there a reason for it?" Antonio said, "I am just happy to be here."

Mary kindly informs him that she is planning to make coffee and cook some eggs. She then extends an invitation, asking if he would like to join Oscar and her for breakfast. Antonio hesitates to answer. Mary tells him, "You don't have to pay for the food here."

He shakes his head up and down, nodding yes.

In the midst of Mary's breakfast preparations, she takes the chance to question Antonio about the purpose of his visit to Tucson. With his reputation for telling long and intriguing stories, he begins his tale of woe that originated from a dream he had about working with his grandfather.

In the doorway behind him, Oscar is leaning against the doorjamb, appearing to be listening politely, unbeknownst to Antonio. In his narrative, he vividly recounts his childhood dreams, shares insights into his life in Mexico, reflects on the influence of his parents, expresses his burning desire to come to America, and narrates his arduous journey.

Despite this, he purposefully chooses not to mention his deep spiritual bond with Luna or the amazing discovery of his secret stash of gold coins.

After Oscar takes his seat at the table, he inquires if there was anything interesting that he might have missed, even though he knows he heard the entire story. They all consumed the scrambled eggs and toast and drank their coffee. They gathered around the table, exuding a sense of familiarity and warmth, as if they had been a close-knit family for sufficient years. Their presence together felt completely natural.

Once the last piece of food had been consumed, Mary took it upon herself to clear the table, while Oscar, on the other hand, declared his intention to go to work and open the pawnshop. Mary had some shopping errands to run. She and Oscar gave Antonio a key to the house before they departed for the day, leaving Antonio in his room.

Since the house is currently vacant and muted, Antonio sees this as the perfect opportunity to conjure up Luna and tell her of his good fortune. However, he would have to wait until evening when the darkness sets in as he has never called upon Luna during the hours of daylight. Instead of doing something else, he will spend today exploring the surrounding area in order to familiarize himself with his current location.

It is unquestionable that this is his first time experiencing the hustle and bustle of an urban city, a completely new environment for him, as he is accustomed to the peacefulness of the farmland.

He has just one change of clothes, a clean tee shirt and jeans. He takes off his grubby traveling attire and places it on the floor of the closet. Then, he gathers some U.S. cash hoping to find a clothing outlet.

As he walks back toward Oscar's pawnshop, he discovers several retail stores lining the path. While passing by a Goodwill Store, a place he had never seen before, he decided to take a peek through the window and was pleasantly surprised to see a wide variety of clothing. Once he decided to step inside, he was greeted by a vast expanse of rows, containing an assortment of clothing items, ranging from shirts and pants to underwear and shoes.

As he rummaged through the racks, he could find not just one, but two pairs of jeans that fit him perfectly. Besides the jeans, he also discovered several tee shirts, including one with the name Tucson printed on it. To complete his shopping spree, he even managed to find a pair of thongs, along with underwear. The total amount he spent on his brand-new wardrobe was $35.00.

As he continued on his journey, he stumbled upon a local park that was swarming with saguaro cacti, vibrant trees, and an abundance of bushes and colorful plants, native to Arizona. As he walked around the parameters of the park, carefully observing every detail, he concluded that this specific location would be absolutely perfect for summoning Luna during the late evening.

Antonino investigated the entire park, ultimately discovering the largest and oldest saguaro tree that had been planted in that specific area. It was an awe-inspiring sight to discover a granddaddy of about twenty feet in height, adorned with eight arms that seemed to stretch endlessly toward the heavens. The central trunk must be three feet in width. The appearance of arms on a saguaro is a characteristic that typically occurs when the cactus reaches a minimum age of fifty to seventy years.

The arms have multiple purposes and serve a variety of functions. The main stem and its arms are responsible for the important function of water storage, particularly during the rainy season. The arms of the plant are responsible for producing both flowers and fruit. The plant has a quality that brings to mind the concept of timelessness. He has now chosen this saguaro to serve as his contact point with Luna.

CHAPTER 5

Upon his return home, he discovers Mary diligently working in the kitchen, preparing delicious beef tacos and eagerly awaiting Oscar's arrival after a long day at work.

Antonio approached Mary and kindly inquired if there was any assistance he could offer while residing in their home. With excitement shining in her eyes, Mary eagerly volunteers to answer without hesitation saying, "Oscar is tired and aging and has been spending excessive hours at the pawnshop. It would be appreciated if you could accompany him to the store and offer him your assistance. Let's discuss this subject during dinner tonight."

Antonio's ability to listen to the wind has allowed him to find answers to nearly every subject, a gift that he has possessed throughout his entire life.

Once Oscar entered, the food was carefully placed on the table at home, and then the three of them took a moment to say grace. Mary suggests to Oscar that it might be a blessing for Antonio to work with him, providing several hours of assistance at the pawnshop.

Oscar's response, which was warmly received, contained an invitation that hinted at the possibility of him imparting his knowledge on the history of the various objects he has collected throughout the years to Antonio. Little did Oscar know about Antonio's secret ability, a power that allowed him to harness his special gift, ultimately leading him to become the one with extensive knowledge. They all agree Antonio will accompany Oscar to work tomorrow.

After dinner, he retreats to his room and lies on his bed, anticipating sunset and the darkness of evening. As the stars turn bright and the sun sets, a full moon appears in the heaven above.

With confident strides, he enters the cozy living room, announcing to Oscar and Mary his intention to take a stroll to the nearby park, where he plans to bask in the enchanting glow of the starlight and savor the delightful fragrance of the evening flowers. A word of caution is given to him regarding the people who visit the park after dark.

Once he arrives at the park, following a brief stroll, he locates the massive saguaro and takes a seat on the vibrant, green grass. With his legs crossed and his head tilted downwards, he immerses himself in deep concentration, his focus fixated on Luna and her captivating emerald eyes.

An hour passes, no signs of Luna, then suddenly an Arizona monsoon starts, wind spinning the leaves on the ground, and rain pouring down relentlessly. Despite being soaked and his clothes drenched, Antonio remains seated, displaying remarkable patience.

As he looks up at the heavens, rain filling his eyes, a lightning flash appears and strikes the saguaro Cactus in front of him, leaving no damage to the plant.

With a mesmerizing sight, the Cactus opens up in front of him, showcasing its archway, adorned with thorns, accompanied by a soothing hum that fills the air.

Luna, with her emerald eyes glowing and her dark, long, wet, and straight hair flowing over her shoulders, stands at the entrance. Her dress dampened by the rain, she extends her arm toward Antonio, leading him into the saguaro chamber.

A large hall of echoing sounds, the center became a coliseum of beauty, shimmering in dewdrops - a beacon radiating life and magic. In the heart of this luminous veil, you can see the sight of ancient trees, leaves shimmering like gold.

As he enters the cactus portals in the quietness of meditation, he feels his body slip into stillness. The saguaro offers a peacefulness dissolving the past and present, the before and after. His feelings have been washed away, leaving behind only the shimmering essence of the present moment, Antonio, and Luna together.

A large hall of echoing sounds became a coliseum of beauty, shimmered in dewdrops, a beacon, radiating life and magic. In the heart of this golden luminous veil, you can see the sight of ancient trees and leaves shimmering like gold.

Antonio was back in the whispering woods, where the winds carry secrets of lost kingdoms, and tales of forgotten days that peer through numerous dimensions. Shooting stars still grant wishes that defy time. Antonio finds Luna could lead him through curtains between worlds and time. She tells Antonio those who step through the Vail find themselves reborn with new courage. They become wanderers and storytellers of the past.

As the portal doors closed, António and Luna found themselves in solitude, providing them with an opportunity to engage in conversation. The secrets that they wanted to share were whispered through their words. Antonio tells of the new family he has found, their generosity, concerns, and love.

Luna explains the blessing he has obtained, and her hopes that he will accept their offerings and return their love. Luna explains Oscar and Mary's desire to have a son, to support them through difficult times, and with Antonio's knowledge, he could help lead them to a better path.

Luna tells him to follow his heart, with her guidance he will discover new desires and accomplishments. She stands and takes him by his hand and leads him through the inner chamber to the open saguaro portal, back to the park where they met.

Taking a moment to sit and reflect on the experience he just encountered, he then stands up and begins walking back to the house, his heart overflowing with a mixture of joy and hope.

Upon returning home, Antonio discovered that Oscar and Mary were already fast asleep, so he quietly made his way to his own room. Upon entering the room, he immediately felt the weight of exhaustion and couldn't resist the urge to collapse onto his bed, flopping onto his back and letting out a long sigh of relief.

Then he opened the window, the cool night air and gentle breeze effortlessly filled his room, creating an atmosphere that seemed to carry whispers from the past, sharing stories of days long gone. As he listened, he could hear the sound of his mother crying, her tears flowing uncontrollably, while she read the note he left behind. He felt the immense emptiness that had taken hold of her, yearning for her only son.

Antonio decided to sit at his desk and pen her a letter about his current health and his good fortune of finding a home in Tucson. He assures her of his unwavering love and expresses his commitment to actively pursue his dreams for the future. After folding the letter, he proceeds to seal the envelope, which he plans to mail tomorrow. As his eyes grow heavy, he succumbs to sleep, while the gentle whispers of the wind enlighten his mind.

He rises early the next morning and proceeds to prepare for work, ensuring he is dressed in his fresh attire. He Joins Oscar and Mary in the kitchen as they eat their breakfast, creating a cozy atmosphere for everyone to enjoy.

Oscar asks, "Are you prepared for a day of work and the opportunity to learn about things that others may not be interested in?" Antonio nods, saying yes.

As they leave the house, both of them walk at a leisurely pace while Oscar takes the opportunity to explain how customers often bring items to the pawnshop that they believe are valuable, without realizing the difference between gold and brass. Just because you have received an old teacup from your grandmother does not imply that it holds any value as a collector's item, it is merely a teacup.

As soon as Oscar arrives at the shop, he immediately lights up the entire facility, proceeds to open the storefront shutters, and turns on the air conditioner to ensure a comfortable environment for customers. While in the shop, Antonio takes the opportunity to carefully observe the various items on display. His attention is drawn to an old wooden ship's steering wheel, made of Teak, which measures about three feet in width.

The moment he takes it off the wall rack, the sounds of the ocean fill his ears, and an image of the vessel it once was guiding emerges, evoking memories of its glorious voyages in years gone by. In his mind, he sees an old wooden cargo boat, perhaps built in the seventeen-hundreds, arriving at a port in Boston, Massachusetts, officially a commonwealth in the Northeastern United States, bordering on the Atlantic Ocean. The cargo that is being transported on the ships comprises bags of tea.

Imagining, he stands on the shore, he can feel the chill of the frosty day and the roughness of the harbor waters, while his eyes take in the sight of American colonists gathering at the harbor. A period when the new colonies were being oppressed by taxes from England. The ship, which had just arrived from East India, was carrying chests filled with tea.

The colonists, refusing to tolerate taxation any longer, sparked a revolution that led to a significant event in history known as the Boston Tea Party. During this event, they dumped all the cargo into the ocean as a powerful act of protest.

When Antonio saw this image, it stirred up emotions in him as he contemplated the countless stories that each piece of merchandise held within Oscar's shop. It is truly astonishing to consider that this historically significant piece was available for purchase at a mere $25.00; Oscar was completely unaware of the true value of his possession. One way in which Antonio could contribute is by utilizing his knowledge to accurately assess the value of the pieces and then facilitating their sale to collectors.

As they both sat behind the counter awaiting their first customer of the day, Antonio took the time to share with Oscar the fascinating history behind the ship's steering wheel. Oscar, naturally, had doubts about the accuracy of the information. After all, how could a sixteen-year-old boy from Mexico possibly possess such knowledge?

Oscar decided to contact the history department at the University of Arizona and engaged in a conversation with the professor. He provided him with information regarding the items that he currently has in his store. The professor was interested in seeing and evaluating its authenticity. The professors holding a high ranking within the educational system are experts in their respective fields.

The following day, Professor Jones from the history department arrived at 9:00 am, along with one of his students. Taking photos, testing the wood for its age, and checking the fragment of sea salt on the steering wheel, they determined Antonio was correct as to the vintage of the ship's wheel. But was it from the Boston Tea Party? Further assessment would have to prove that the tea from India was enlarged in its wood, along with the saltwater from the Atlantic Ocean.

Oscar and Antonio agreed to let the professor take the ship's wheel back to the university lab and do further testing on its surface.

The afternoon seemed to fly by as they had a customer who came in intending to sell a silver vase. Oscar bought it for a price of $10.00 and positioned it in the exact spot where the ship's wheel used to be located. During supper later that evening, Oscar and Antonio took the opportunity to share with Mary the exciting discovery they had made. She lacked a significant amount of interest in the events of the pawnshop, it was a business of no importance to her.

As Antonio enters his room after supper, he opens the window, inviting the soft gentle breeze to enter, and in that moment, a poignant emotion tugs at his heartstrings. The feeling of being separated from your family or finding yourself in an unfamiliar place is an emotion that many can relate to. When you find yourself in a state of uncertainty, it is natural to question the decisions you have made and whether they align with what is right.

As he lay in bed, unable to fall asleep, he found solace in listening to the gentle breeze whispering secrets of the unique opportunities that were destined for him. Starting is crucial, and what better place to start than here, with a loving family who is yearning to welcome you into their hearts? As the gentle malady is sung by the winds, his eyes begin to grow heavy and he falls into a peaceful slumber.

CHAPTER 6

The following day, around noon, Professor Jones arrives at the shop with the ship's wheel wrapped carefully in a brown parchment paper. He asks both Oscar and Antonio to please have a seat. He has an important proposal for them.

He said, "After testing, we found embedded in the wood both salt from the Atlantic and microparticles of tea that came from the West Indies. The ship "The Dartmouth," commanded by Captain James Hall, was the first tea ship to arrive in Boston. And yes, we believe this is the steering wheel of the ship."

The joy and excitement of the news brought a tear to Oscar's eye.

The professor continued. "The university is interested in showcasing this artifact in its esteemed history department. Moreover, they would like to acknowledge you, Oscar, as the generous donor, and recognize your shop for its invaluable contribution. Furthermore, as a token of gratitude, the university is pleased to offer you a payment of $1,000 for your support towards enriching our museum. Are you interested?"

Oscar's immediate response, with no hesitation, is a booming "Yes."

Both Oscar and Antonio, working together as a team, successfully established a reputable name for the pawnshop. This resulted in significant profits for the store and earned them a high level of respect within the community. A day to close early and celebrate.

Oscar takes Antonio to the park after stopping at the sandwich shop for food. They proceed to the park where they find a table in a muted corner, under a large tree and Oscar begins to tell Antonio of his past.

Telling Antonio that his parents were farm workers in Mexico before they came to Arizona, bringing with them a son of five-year-old. Both he and Mary had ambitious plans to open a vegetable market, acquire a piece of land, and cultivate and sell organic produce. Despite his initial plans not panning out, he ended up becoming a junk collector, which ultimately paved the way for him to establish a pawn shop, using the various items he had accumulated – a true fork in the road.

Mary, who was a young wife at the time, worked diligently in the kitchen of a Taco food outlet, where she skillfully prepared a variety of delicious Mexican dishes for valued customers. Having worked as a short-order cook for fifteen years, she decided to leave her job when her son fell ill and has not worked since.

Antonio, who has always harbored the desire to open a bar and cafe just like his grandfather did, now finds himself distracted by his intuitive ability and his unique communication with the wind and nature that surround him. When torn between two desires, it is not an effortless task to make a decision, but having the guidance of a spirit named Luna certainly helps. After spending several hours sharing their deepest desires with each other, they decided it was time to head home for dinner and both walked together.

Both individuals were engrossed in their own thoughts, contemplating the conversations that had just transpired, and how it related to them. When the evening arrived, Oscar generously offers to share his newfound payment with Antonio, who kindly declines the funds and requests that the money be given to Mary instead. Being cognizant of the fact that he has a small fortune in gold hidden in his room, he is careful not to reveal this secret to anyone.

Later that evening when Oscar and Mary were asleep, Antonio made his way quietly to the park to speak with Luna. He proceeds with his ritual before the giant sequoia cactus, awaiting Luna to appear. As the lightning cracks and strikes the cactus, an extraordinary event occurs - the entrance to the sequoia opens up before him, revealing a breathtaking sight. In that moment, he is greeted by the ethereal presence of Luna, gleaming and displaying her majestic beauty in all its glory. Once more, she reaches out to him, gently clasping his hand as she leads him towards the grand sacred coliseum hall. There, they find themselves in the company of majestic ancient trees, their presence enhanced by a luminous veil that shimmers brightly, resembling the precious metal gold.

Antonio decided to confide in Luna, expressing his anxiety and dilemma about whether to continue pursuing his original dream or embark on a different path. Luna, who is an expert in the subject, takes the time to explain it thoroughly saying, "Just like a vast landscape, your emotions encompass various terrains, valleys, peaks, and even hidden springs waiting to be explored. One way to begin exploring your emotions is by starting with the simple act of naming them. It would be beneficial for you to take a moment and engage in some self-reflection, focusing on your emotions and attempting to pinpoint the exact emotion you are presently feeling.

Are you feeling joy, sadness, anger, or curiosity? It is important to acknowledge them passing no judgment. Your body acts as a compass, providing emotional markers through your physical sensations that you should pay attention to. It is important to develop the ability to understand and empathize with the emotions of others. By listening to the wind, you can find guidance that will lead you toward fulfillment.

Antonio, it is important to remember that emotions should not be seen as enemies. Use these guides as a resource to help you shape and mold your journey in a way that aligns with your goals and aspirations."

Luna, with a gentle motion, leans forward and gracefully pushes the veil aside. With excessive tenderness, she leans forward and places a gentle kiss on Antonio's head, symbolizing her deep desire to give a heartfelt blessing to him. Taking her hand, she confidently leads him towards the portal doors, and as he walks out, a sense of enlightenment washes over him, providing him with a clearer grasp of what steps to follow.

Upon returning to his bedroom, he takes a moment to open his window, then he leisurely lies down on the bed to listen to the soothing whispers of the warm wind. Because the wind's sound has not disappointed him thus far, he is inspired to dig even deeper into their innermost being.

Considering his recent experiences and newfound skills, he carefully evaluates them alongside his lifelong dream, giving significant consideration to both.

At breakfast the next day, Antonio confides in Oscar about his aspiration to wander through the vibrant urban streets of Tucson, envisioning the possibilities of owning a bar and cafe in the future. Oscar asks if he wants company, and he tells Oscar it is something he needs to do alone.

As he takes a short walk downtown, he cannot help but notice the deterioration of the inner city and the immense number of homeless vagrants camping outside of stores. Passing a bar and grill with outside seating, he sits and occupies a table and orders a taco. He notices business is slow to non-existent.

As the owner brought him his food, he asked, "How is business, and would you be hiring help?"

The owner told him," It is so slow he has to wash his own customer's dishes and cook himself."

That response burst Antonio's bubble on owning a Café in Tucson. Thinking back to last night's conversation with Luna about listening to his emotions, he decides to try the new path, using his special abilities to discover and conjure up memories and facts about the past.

The fact that he now views the chance to work with Oscar as a blessing is bringing him a successful sense of joy and happiness. This could be the answer he was seeking from Luna, trusting his inner feelings.

Perhaps Oscar and Mary are his special gifts, giving him the valuable gift of time and the gift to choose. Luna gives him the gift of special moments, listening, giving him direction and encouragement. Weaving all this together is priceless.

On his way home, just after noon, he stops at the pawnshop, sits with Oscar and they speak about the future. Antonio reveals to Oscar his ability to listen to the wind, and conjure events and stories of the past as he did with the ship's steering wheel. Oscar's disbelief in the fantasy remains, even though he had a direct experience with the ship's wheel.

Oscar, in a gesture of goodwill, offers Antonio an olive branch and proposes that if Antonio can uncover the historical background of another item, Oscar will grant him a partnership in the pawnshop. His efforts in relieving pressure and implementing effective strategies played a crucial role in turning the business around.

Oscar is going above and beyond by suggesting that he and Antonio divide the profits equally, besides everything else. With his emotions stirred up by his conversation with Luna, he decided to trust his instincts and eagerly seize the opportunity. The future holds promise, with the advent of a new door opening.

So now, on this rainy afternoon, as droplets rhythmically bounced on the storefront window, a seed was planted and a bond became evident between them both. A gray-haired older man with twinkling eyes entered, holding a box. When asked if he needed help, he opened the box to reveal an old, musty-smelling book, with half its pages written and the rest blank. Oscar asked what he wanted to do with the old journal and the old man replied, "Sell it."

When he discovered the journal in his attic, he was surprised to find that it contained a collection of forgotten tales, all of which were meticulously written with a quill pen. Some narratives capture the essence of past escapades and remarkable travels. Although the author remains unknown, the stories within the book are filled with tales of adventure from the past, depicting life in the Old West, and capturing the essence of embracing new beginnings and overcoming the challenges of that era.

Although the author of the book is unknown, Oscar explained it had no value, but emphasized the distinctive nature of its passages. The gray-haired man requested twenty dollars for the journal.

Looking to his left, Antonio nodded as if to say purchase the book.

Once the customer departed, Antonio will be taking the book home tonight and plans to delve into its depths to uncover the identity of its author. After dinner, he went to his room, opened the window, laid on his bed, the journal resting on his chest. He listened intently to the whisper of the winds, he could hear the conflict of war and guns firing in his ears.

The perception he had was that this journal had been penned amidst a battle which could plausibly explain its unfinished state. Yet, the lingering question remained: who was the author? It is evident from the parchment pages, which exude an air of antiquity and elegance, that they must have been penned by an individual of elevated authority in the stations of life.

Personal diaries were a common practice among soldiers during the Civil War, serving as a means for them to record their daily lives and provide firsthand accounts of the hardships and experiences they faced. But who had penned this journal in its unique elegance of handwriting, perhaps old English? The writer was well educated and used an elaborate letter form, judging from the letter style and presentation.

While lying on his bed pondering and hearing the sound that surrounded the book while being penned, a flash of light appeared in the open window. Turning to look at what caused this distraction, there was Luna, with her emerald eyes aglow.

Antonio was astounded, Luna had never come to visit him, he would always go to her. She asked Antonio to take her hand and she would take him to the time and moment that the journal was written. Flabbergasted, he does as she asks. Placing his hand in hers, they levitate into the heavens, above tall mountains, entering large white clouds. The earth looked like a small blue marble. Vast oceans of blue dominated the planet. Amidst the blue water, patches of brown, yellow, and green emerge.

Each continent tells a story, a tapestry of cultures and history. Returning to the earth, clouds dance across the earth's atmosphere forming an intricate pattern and casting shadows on the land below. As they descend, overlooking a brown, dirty tent in the western desert, they spot General Armstrong Custer, a distinguished army officer of the cavalry, who graduated from West Point. At present, he can be seated on a sleeping cot, completely absorbed in writing as he reflects on a poignant moment that occurred during the war. He along with the members of his troops are currently stationed near the majestic Bighorn River in the vast Montana Territory.

Luna acknowledged the journal he was writing in was indeed the unfinished memories of General Custer. He made sure to never sign his name, as he did not want the enemy to discover his true identity.

Despite everything, Luna, his guardian spirit, was by his side as they witnessed the military slaughter and observed the entire sequence of events leading up to General Custer's demise.

The vivid images, powerful scents, and tactile sensations of the battlefield became deeply ingrained in his memory, creating an unforgettable experience.

Luna returned Antonio to his room back home, where his mind danced among the stars in a cosmic theater. Like shining stars, each vision he has encountered through his experiences illuminates his knowledge of the journal he was holding.

The next morning, while sitting at the kitchen table, he recounted his experience to Oscar and shared the intriguing details he had uncovered about the enigmatic, unfinished journal. Oscar suggested calling professor Jones and bringing the journal to his attention, and so they did.

In the afternoon, professor Jones arrived at the pawnshop where he was handed the journal that had been found. The professor carefully examined each page of the ancient parchment paper, meticulously evaluating the type of ink that was used. In order to authenticate its originality, Oscar, and Antonio were informed that the University would need to conduct tests on the paper, ink, and handwriting.

Several of the pages at the beginning of the journal were clear and read,

"When I investigated the matters on the spot directly after the Indians vacated the village, I discovered that they had burned a mail station on Smokey Hill, killed the white man stationed there, and disemboweled and burned his body."

This excerpt provides the challenges and conflicts faced during Custer's time on the plains. The empty following pages were not completed because of Custer's death during the battle it is assumed.

Once again, Professor Jones, filled with eagerness to uncover the historical significance of this writing, is eager to expedite the authentication process for the handwriting, ink, and paper. While Antonio is carefully wrapping the journal, he accidentally slips and utters a few words.

"It is indeed real as I witnessed him writing the journal just last night."

The professor stops dead in his tracks while exiting, turns to Antonio, and says,

"You witnessed him writing this last night?"

Knowing he made a mistake saying that he added,

"In my dreams."

To witch the professor replies,

"I hope you are correct; it would be another wonder piece to add to our museum collection." And he leaves.

CHATER 7

Upon arriving home, Antonio received a letter from Mexico. In it, his mother informed him that his father was ill with an unusual disease. She explained that it was a zoonotic disease, transmitted from horses, which is extremely rare but can be risky for those who have close contact with an infected horse. Rabies, specifically, can be transmitted through a horse's saliva if it comes into contact with a minor cut.

His mom is requesting financial help for medical costs, which Antonio can certainly provide from his gold coin collection. He tells Oscar of the event and tells Oscar he has another coin he can sell to send the money to his parents.

Oscar took Antonio to a jewelry store that buys gold, where he was offered $1,500 for the coin. He accepted the offer, purchased a money order with the funds, and immediately sent it to his mother in Mexico. His actions reflect his genuine love for his parents.

Upset by the news of his father's illness, Antonio went to the park that evening to seek Luna's guidance. As the sun sets and the skies turn to darkness, he waits in front of the giant saguaro cactus calling upon the spirit of Luna to appear.

Without the bust of lightning, the portal doors of the cactus opened, and Luna appeared before him. She extended her hand, inviting him into the grand chamber. They sat behind golden veils, and Antonio shared his deep concern for his father.

A hush fell over the chamber, the silence profound. Suddenly, a great fire erupted, reaching toward the heavens. Luna told Antonio about the legendary Tree of Life, whose leaves could cure any ailment. She stood, took his hand, and led him into the shadows, embarking with him on their journey to find the magical tree.

The journey took them through undeserved valleys, and crossing mountaintops, guided by the stars and the whispers of the wind. As they made their way through the thick, white clouds, the path they traveled was fraught with numerous challenges, making their journey up the peaks of the mountains even more arduous.

As they approached the majestic Tree of Life, they reached out to pluck several leaves, which were the ripe and luscious fruit of the tree's branches. With the blessings given to them by the leaves and the great spirit, they made their way back to the portal of the saguaro cactus. Antonio is instructed by Luna to send the sacred leave to his father, understanding that consuming it would allow the great spirit of the Tree of Life to work its healing powers and cure his ailments.

Thanking Luna for her help and blessing, Antonio returned home to write a note and place the spiritual leave in an envelope to mail off to his mother. Now, he could only wait and hope for her acknowledgment of the results.

Opening his window to listen to the whispering winds, he could see images of his ill fathers lying in the home's bedroom. The more he became absorbed in his vision, the stronger his sensation of hovering above his Mexican residence became, granting him a panoramic view of the ongoing occurrences below. He realized he could transport his image to another location without Luna's assistance.

The nightly warm breeze advised him to seek the identity of each object in the pawnshop, there were other finding awaiting his discovery.

The next morning, filled with anticipation and excitement, he hurriedly made his way to the shop, carefully examining and appreciating every piece, taking the time to hold each one individually, immersing himself in the history and essence of each item.

Among the items discovered during the search were salt and pepper shakers that had been passed down through generations of relatives, elegant silver vases that had once graced the family's dining table with beautiful flowers, and even discarded junk that had been mistakenly cast off as trash.

Several uneventful days later, Professor Jones visited the shop, a smile on his long thin face, mustached trimmed, wearing a gray sports jacket and saying,

"I have extraordinary news for you. All the tests, paper, ink, and handwriting came back positive, the journal was in fact the beginning of a writing by General Custer. The history department is prepared to make you the same offer and name your business on a dedication plack, as we did with the ship's wheel, Oscar, do you have an interest?"

In a more considerate manner, Oscar replies,

"I will need to discuss it with my partner, Antonio first, can we get back to you this afternoon?"

The professor left the journal wrapped protectively on the counter and said, "We will speak later."

Opening a brown paper bag, given to them by Mary upon leaving the house for work, they find two sandwiches, two bags of chips, and two apples. Oscar walked over to the door and turned the open sign to the closed position. They sit at the counter to discuss Professor Jones's proposal.

The pros, receive a respectable size check and another pawn shop affirmation. Cons, None.

Antonio says,

"The presence of two items being exhibited at the museums will probably attract a larger number of customers in search of collectibles that are not meant to be used, leading to an increase in our business."

Once they have finished their lunch, they proceed to reach out to Professor Jones to inform him of their acceptance regarding the agreement with the proposal. Antonio's next task on his to-do list involves taking home an item from the pawnshop every night and attempting to uncover any intriguing stories or history associated with it. A gift he has that came naturally to him.

Tonight, he eagerly takes home an ancient Indian bow that is made of worn and splitting wood. Additionally, the bow's attachment to animal tendons is missing, most likely decaying from its old age. While he listens to the wind, it softly whispers to him about the bow and arrow, a combination that has stood the test of time and has been embraced by countless cultures and continents.

The bow is composed of either wood or horn, and its limbs can store elastic energy when they are flexed. The bowstring serves as a connection between the ends of the bow.

Lying on his bed with the bow resting across his chest, he starts to fall asleep. In his dream, he sees an ancient Indian warrior holding a bow, sitting atop a large white horse. While Arizona is home to many Native American tribes, Ak-Chin, Havasupai, and the most notable the Navajo Nation, the largest reservation in the United States. Covering Arizona, and New Mexico.

One of the most famous Navajo Indians is Manuelito, his legacy interwoven with the Navajo people. Despite the demands of the U.S. government, he staunchly refused to surrender and instead chose to retreat into the mountains, where he engaged in guerrilla warfare with the Calvary.

Upon awakening, he suddenly became aware that the winds had bestowed upon him the knowledge of the Bow's history, which carried immense historical significance.

A wave of excitement washed over him, like an electric current, filling his entire being and consuming every fiber of his body. With his heart quickening and his lungs expanding, he feels a surge of energy coursing through his body. Once again, like in previous instances, he has stumbled upon yet another extraordinary historical artifact that serves to enhance his ever-growing collection of found objects.

After just a few moments, a noticeable shift occurs in his mood, as his thoughts transport him back to his initial aspiration of owning his own business like his grandfather's Bar and Grill. As the soft, warm light breeze gently caresses him, it lulls him into a deep and thoughtful slumber.

As the morning sunshine gently pours into his eyes, its comforting warmth delicately embraces his face, and as his eyes slowly awaken, he discovers himself immersed in a mesmerizing spectacle - a myriad of stunning butterflies, each displaying vibrant hues from the entire spectrum of the rainbow.

The sensation he experiences feels like being enveloped in a cocoon of sheer beauty. As he swings his legs over the side of the bed to rise, he is greeted by the sight of the window filled with a mesmerizing display of departing dancing butterflies. As he sat at the edge of the bed, he could not help but wonder what this signal meant.

Since it has been a month, he will need to make a decision soon between pursuing his dream of opening a bar and grill or embarking on the new adventure that Luna has presented to him. As long as he continues to follow Luna's guidance, his love, and attachment to her will endure, but if he cannot do so, he may end up losing her. His trust and faith in her has expanded so much that it now transcends the boundaries of the universe.

Along with the love of a new family, she has given upon him the companionship and devotion of Oscar, a dedicated friend, and partner. He has filled the void in Mary's heart caused by the loss of her son, bringing her comfort and solace. Antonio never brought up the subject of how both Oscar and Mary lost their son.

At the breakfast table that morning, he decided to ask Mary the sensitive question,

"What happened to Juan?"

As Mary sits at the table, a tear begins to form in her eyes, and she proceeds to tell Antonio that he was born with leukemia, which is a type of cancer that affects the blood cells and tragically claims the lives of individuals before they reach the age of fifteen. The struggles that he endured were incredibly heartbreaking. Once he eventually passed away, her interest in her own life diminished completely as she continued to grieve for losing Juan. It has been impossible for her to erase the heart-breaking event from her life, even after all this time has passed. Despite being told by numerous people to move on, she finds it impossible to do so.

At that moment, Antonio made a firm decision to approach Luna during their next encounter and discuss with her the possibility of finding a solution to assist Mary in accepting the loss and easing the pain caused by the passing of Juan.

Shortly after the mail was delivered to the house, Antonio received a letter from his mother. She told him "His father at the special magical leaf from the tree of life, he had sent and the following day his illness was cured."

When Antonio heard this wonderful news, it ignited a spark within him and gave him even more conviction in his belief in Luna's powers. Once he had placed the letter in his room, he quickly made his way to the pawnshop to join Oscar for work and eagerly shared the good news with him. Miracles can happen.

The afternoon at the pawnshop was rather uneventful, with Oscar busy perching some collectable stamps and managing to sell a guitar along with two old watches.

Antonio, upon arriving home that evening after a long day at work, took some time to reflect on his earlier conversation with Mary over breakfast. Later that evening, he decided to take a leisurely walk to the park in order to have a conversation with Luna, hoping to seek help and find relief for Mary.

The darkness and humidity of the evening signaled the arrival of Tucson's tropical summer monsoon, which could be felt in the air.

In a serene setting, Antonio finds solace in the presence of the magnificent saguaro cactus, as he assumes a seated position, crossing his legs and bowing his head in contemplation, his mind fixated on the enchanting appearance of Luna and her striking emerald eyes.

Soon in the night's silence, the cactus portal doors open, and before him, a pronounced white light and the image of Luna appeared. Reaching for Antonio's hand, she says, "I invite you to join me in the private chamber, where we can have a conversation about your concern. Antonio, I understand you are not present here for your personal benefit, but for the sake of someone you deeply care about. In what ways can I be of assistance to you?"

Antonio tells Luna of the misfortune of Rosa's son and her loss, along with how she could not shed the grief. Luna Says,

"Come with me and I will lead you to a serene spot nestled in the heart of the ancient forest, where the gentle sunlight cascades through the shimmering golden leaves, and where a majestic willow tree stands tall with its branches stretching towards the heavens."

Explaining this tree is no ordinary tree, it is a keeper of memories. The local villages called it the whispering Willow, for it held grief throughout the generations. When sorrow weighed heavy upon the hearts, they sought solace beneath its weeping branches.

Visitors would come and whisper their grieving secrets, and the pain that pooled their eyes with tears. Antonio asks, "Why does love bring so much pain?"

Luna explains in a soft voice, "Because love is the echo of eternity, it blinds souls."

Antonio asks, "But how do we eliminate the ache?"

Luna responds by saying, "You already know the answer. Just listen to the wind, for it carries the echoes of all those who have loved and lost.

Upon your return, it is crucial that you take the time to explain the situation to Mary, allowing her to truly feel her grief, surrender to it, accept what has happened, and find the strength to cross over the bridge."

Upon leaving the Saguaro portal, Antonio heads home, meditating over what Luna has proposed and contemplating a way to execute the plan.

The next morning, as Mary and Antonio sat down for breakfast together, Oscar had already left for work. Antonio, with a gentle gesture, leaned across the table to reach out and touch Mary's hand, his unwavering gaze fixated on her captivating large brown eyes, as though he was fervently yearning for a profound connection with the depths of her soul.

The moment came, Mary looked back with a grazed covering her eyes. She remained silent, listening attentively as Antonio elaborated on the process of crossing the bridge by acknowledging the events of the past and embracing new experiences in the future.

Saying, "Remember to grant yourself forgiveness, as the responsibility does not lie with you but with the unfaltering faith of the gods, which we have no control."

Antonio continues to speak to Mary, explaining that deep within the chambers of her heart, where emotions dance and twirl like leaves caught in a gentle breeze, the truth resides and it rises above any sense of blame. The fault does not rest upon you; rather, it is the four simple words that can bring about healing. "It is not your fault."

Mary, feeling a mix of confusion and bewilderment, slowly gets up from the table and heads towards her room, where she intends to find solace by closing the door and being alone.

Antonio, full of enthusiasm, begins his day by heading off to work at the pawnshop, eager to find new adventures and experiences. Prior to his departure from the house, he took a moment to return to his bedroom and retrieve the bow of Manuelito, a Navajo Indian, which he intended to bring back to the shop.

Upon his arrival at the store, Oscar was seen leisurely enjoying his morning by sitting down, sipping on a cup of coffee, and indulging in a delicious cherry Danish. He noticed the eager expression on Antonio's face, as he eagerly awaited the news of the exciting discovery that had been made. Following a brief conversation, they reached a mutual decision that it would be most beneficial to keep the artifact.

To enhance its educational significance, they decided to affix a label beneath it, offering a brief account of its historical context and potential ownership. In addition, placing a price tag of $ 1,500 on the item. Would they get an offer?

CHAPTER 8

Antonio, to keep himself occupied, decided to search through the storage room at the back of the store, hoping to discover peculiar objects that might convey a message from a bygone era. What he found that day was an overwhelming amount of dust and numerous cardboard boxes in a state of decay.

When we both returned home for supper that evening, Antonino discovered, Mary was working in the kitchen with a smile and appeared to be happy. When Mary saw Oscar, she walked over to him and gave him a hug and kiss on the cheek, saying, "My two men are home."

As dinner was placed on the table, Mary found herself with so much to discuss, which was quite unusual in their home. She inquired how our day was, and if we acquired any new objects or sold any of the inventory. I told her of the Navajo Bow, and her reaction was a pleasant surprise. She has completely changed her attitude towards the pawnshop, which is a complete reversal of her previous views. Mary's attitude underwent a noticeable change, and even Oscar noted her impressive comeback.

While Mary continues to speak, she mentions to Oscar that throughout the years, she has taken various items from the shop that caught her attention and stored them in the attic. Once we have finished eating, she will bring them down so that we can evaluate them at our convenience. Oscar looks over at me quietly saying, "Is this Mary?"

Once the table had been cleared and the dishes put away, Oscar and I made our way to the living room to relax and watch TV. Suddenly, we were startled by the sound of footsteps coming from the attic above us.

It is my assumption that we will witness the collection that Mary has amassed over the years soon. We are looking forward to these additional items as they will enhance what we have in the shop now.

As she makes her way down from the attic, a sense of anticipation fills the room. With the cardboard box securely in her grasp, she positions it on the coffee table in front of us. The lid is then lifted, unveiling a fascinating assortment of items, each one meticulously encased in newspaper.

    The first article is removed as she showed us a stunning French candlestick holder. Its presents bore the fragrance of forgotten evenings, holding whispered secrets, and the flicker of countless flames.

    The candle holder, which is made from gilded bronze, has a surface that bears the patina of centuries. The unique shape of each curve reveals a tale of its own. The base of the structure had clawed feet, giving the impression that they were firmly planted in the ground like an eagle fiercely gripping the earth with its sharp claws. The upward spiral of the stem was beautifully decorated with leaves. The beauty of this artwork is truly obvious, and Mary is well aware of it.

At the base a drip tray awaiting melting wax, one could imagine it gracing the table of a Nobel Frenchman. But who?

After hours of adoring this magnificent work of art, I decided to take it into my room, open my window, and call upon the whispers of the wind to help me identify the piece. My ears were brushed by the gentle warmth of the wind, yet it brought no audible sounds to my attention. I found the examination to be overwhelming as I was determined to uncover its origins.

Despite the late hour, I decided to place the candlestick under my jacket and venture to the park in order to seek Luna's assistance. Arriving at the giant saguaro, I sat patiently visualizing Luna and her emerald eyes. The lightning cracks, the Cactus portal doors opened, and Luna appeared. Following her lead, I took her hand and together we made our way to the large enchanted hall. Once there, we found our seats behind the golden screens that floated gently in the breeze, Luna asked,

"Antonio, how can I help you?"

I remove the elegant bronze candlestick holder from under my jacket, handing it to her, asking,

"Do you know who this beautiful artifact belonged to?"

With a graceful movement, Luna reached out and delicately took hold of the piece, her emerald eyes shutting as she began to meditate, lost in her thoughts for a moment. She says yes, would you like to see where it came from, let me take you on a journey to another world."

In a matter of seconds, we found ourselves soaring upwards, ascending towards the heavenly realm, gliding effortlessly through ethereal white clouds that adorned the twilight sky. Imagine walking across a magnificent bridge, glowing with radiant light, that stretches across both the earthly grounds and the vastness of the cosmos. As it floats high above the vast expanse of the ocean, it gradually starts descending, preparing to touch down on a foreign land.

Our feet touch the ground, Luna, tells me we are at the opulent halls of the Chateau de Versailles, with lavish mirrors reflecting the grandeur of the era. The halls were adorned with a luxurious array of silks and lace, creating a visually stunning atmosphere.

Upon entering the Chateau, one cannot help but be captivated by the striking collection of paintings that depict battles from bygone eras, adorning its walls. When we enter the grand dining room, our eyes are immediately drawn to the magnificent table that stretches across the room, offering a variety of seating options. There are multiple candlestick holders on the table, all of which are replicas of the one we held. Luna tells me,

"This chateau is the glory of the 18th century, if you are quiet enough, you can hear the echoes of laughter within the walls.

The candlestick holder that you currently have in your possession was once possessed by King Louis XIV, who was famously known as the Sun King. So, my dear, continue to ask, seek, and knock on strange doors for those actions that unfold the wisdom and revelation of life."

As Luna tightly grips my hand, my heart races with excitement as we embark on our journey back to the saguaro in the park. When we arrive, I exit the portal of the cactus and make my way home, after just completing a journey halfway around the world.

With the hour growing late, I slowly make my way towards my room. Once inside, I take a moment to carefully place the candlestick holder on my dresser. After that, I eagerly open my window, craving the comforting sounds of the winds.

Recently, I have noticed a shift in my aspirations where I no longer yearn to be a Bar and Café owner but have developed an inclination towards exploring the unknown. I am filled with an insatiable thirst for adventure that cannot be quenched. Deep within me lies a profound emotion, a force that drives our dreams, ambitions, and the path we choose to follow.

My current motivation stems from a profound and intense aspiration for something meaningful, whether it be acquiring valuable possessions or engaging in impactful emotional encounters. At seventeen, I, Antonio, am undergoing a transformative journey as I transition into adulthood, embracing the responsibility of making my own decisions confidently and with no hesitation. Despite this, I still rely on Luna for her assistance and guidance.

The following morning, both Oscar and Mary are seated at the kitchen table having breakfast as I emerge from my room, candlestick holder in hand. Oscar asked,

"You took it to sleep with you?"

I begin to share with them the fascinating history that I have learned from the whispers of the winds, as well as the intriguing origins of the candlestick holder. Both questioning my source and accountability. Mary's suggestion is for us to take the artifact to a certified antique dealer located in Phoenix, where they can authenticate the item. We all agree.

Mary's determination to find the perfect place led her to explore various options online, and eventually, she discovered a glowing recommendation for Scottsdale Antique and Estate Sales in Phoenix. Taking action, she proceeds to contact and schedule an appointment for an appraisal at 2:00 pm. Without warning, Mary has reconsidered and is now fully supportive of the pawnshop business.

We all prepare for the two-hour ride and decide to leave at 11:00 am. The drive will take us through the heart of the Arizona Desert, revealing both the beauty and historical landmarks. I am eager to go on the trip, it will be my first adventure to Phoenix.

During the ride, unfolds a canvas of cacti, mesas of sand, and open skies. Along the way, Mary indicates numerous landmarks, including the Picacho Peak Park, Casa Grande Ruins. In the distance, when nearing Phoenix, I could see the urban energy of the city. Tall modern buildings reaching up to the heavens.

The planes are circling the Sky Harbor Airport, creating a bustling scene with the constant flow of auto traffic. While cruising through the city, I made a spontaneous decision to roll down the window of the car, allowing the warm desert wind to tousle my hair and fill my lungs with the enticing aroma of the urban environment.

Upon arriving promptly at our assigned appointment time, the receptionist introduced us to Mr. William King, a certified antique appraiser having a deep understanding of historical artifacts and collectables. Mr. King, dressed in a gray suit, and having a short white mustache, and balding head, greeted us with surprising enthusiasm, looking forward to seeing our candlestick holder.

He explains as a professional, he has a historical understanding of vintage items. The ability to recognize and distinguish genuine antiques from replicas. He distinguishes the craftmanship of each piece, by examining it closely, looking at wear, damage, and any restoration. Telling us he stays current on most items sold. He compares the current items sold to obtain a value.

Inquiring how we discovered it wears bouts, Mary explained that approximately ten years ago, a gentleman came into the pawn shop looking to sell the piece, Oscar purchased it and she liked it so much that she stored it in her attic, and it was forgotten about.

By carefully examining the antique with a magnifying glass, diligently searching through several reference books, and conducting tests on the brass stand, you can thoroughly investigate its origins and authenticity. The process of testing the patina is instrumental in establishing the chronological significance of the item. The current method used by appraisers to test bronze involves the application of voltammetry of microparticles.

Behind the closed door in the back of his store, Mr. King discreetly takes the candlestick holder and proceeds to conduct a test. To summarize, an independent appraiser can be seen as a detective who unravels the mysteries of history.

With him, he brings a selection of books showcasing photographs of items resembling it from that specific time period, and he confidently asserts that it is without a doubt an artifact from the 1800s.

However, the question of who possessed it at that specific time remained unanswered, a mystery that only Antonio, through his travels with Luna, held the key to.

Prior to our departure, we made the payment for the appraisal, which turned out to be quite expensive, totaling $500.00. During the appraisal, we discovered that the candlestick holder was actually, an original French bronze object dating back to the 1800s. However, Mr. King's search for any links to its previous ownership proved futile.

During our drive back to Tucson, we all agreed it would be worth an excessive amount more if we could prove who owned it in the past. Mr. Kings, current evaluation was between $5,000 and $7,000. If a famous name were to be associated with the piece, there is a possibility that the amount could double or even triple. At this moment, the item will be returned to the attic until we can gather additional evidence.

CHAPTER 9

In the evening, as we all gathered around the comfortable living room sofa, engaged in a lively exchange of stories from our past, I made the decision to share with both Oscar and Mary the thrilling tale of my adventure involving the map that I had discovered prior to my arrival in America. I followed the trail and its markings, which eventually led me to a deserted old adobe nestled between the majestic mountains.

There were originally twenty gold coins that were found, and I currently still possess eighteen of them. With a smile on his face, Oscar looks at me and bursts out saying,
"It crossed my mind when we first met to inquire about the whereabouts from which you acquired the gold coin you intended to sell, but I didn't."

Continuing, "Antonio you don't have eighteen coins, you have nineteen. I kept the original one you sold me, and I am going to give it back to you. There is so much you have done for our family, I would feel too much guilt if I remained in possession of the coin."

As Antonio approached the kitchen table the following morning, he was surprised to find a gold coin placed right beside his plate. Throughout several months, the bond between Oscar and Antonio strengthened into something resembling that of a father and son.

The day passed quickly and uneventfully, several customers came in to pawn a watch and rig for some extra cash. Oscar makes them a loan, knowing they will never come back and reclaim their items. When the thirty days pass, he will put them up for sale, hoping to make a small profit.

Following dinner that evening, Antonio takes the time to write a heartfelt letter to his mother, inquiring about the well-being of both her and his father.

While lying in bed on that eventful evening, he listened to the wind whispering long-forgotten secrets to him. As the ethereal breeze delicately swirls around, it carries with it soft whispers that serve as counsel, enlightening us with their profound powers and wisdom. Tonight, Antonio is compelled by the whispers of the wind to delve into the depths of ancient history books, hoping to discover illustrations depicting the mighty leaders of yesteryears.

The following day, while Antonia rummaged through the numerous items in the pawnshop, removing the dirt and dust, he found an old history book containing sketches of old Rome and French leaders of the past. From Ceaser, Mark Antony, Napoléon, and guess who King Louis XIV.

Antonio believes it is by the grace of Luna that King Louis is portrayed in the artwork, standing proudly next to his dining table, with the image of a candlestick holder positioned to his left. The drawing of the antique is the same image as their candlestick holder. With a sense of urgency, he quickly made his way to the front of the shop, loudly calling for Oscar's name as he ran to the front of the shop, saying,

"In this old history book, I could find the proof that we have been searching for, take a look?"

After examining it closely, Oscar noticed that the drawing on the weather page bears a striking resemblance to the shape of the candlestick holder. Both individuals are excited and enthusiastic about sharing this page with both Mary and Mr. King. This drawing will secure their pot of gold.

Closing for lunch, they both hurry home to show Mary Antonio's findings and to call Mr. King. When they reach him by phone, Mary informs him of the history book, publication date, and page number that depicts the antique.

While Mr. King is busy conducting research on the publication of the book and comparing it to the photo of the candlestick he has, he would like to ask Mary to await his call back. With a sense of excitement and eager anticipation, we sat at the kitchen table, watching as the minutes dragged on, feeling like an eternity.

The phone rings, Mary answers and is told the information is correct, she tells the others. In his effort to determine its value, Mr. King stated he would be reaching out to multiple auctioneers and antique collectors.

Receiving good news is like stumbling upon a hidden treasure, instantly filling your heart with joy and brightness. This feeling is like a radiant glow emanating from deep within, casting its light upon your mind and spirit.

While Antonio sits in a peaceful state of meditation, he realizes the immense joy and happiness that has entered his life, prompting him to reflect on his previous objective of serving drinks at a bar. In the depths of his thoughts, he murmurs quietly to himself.

"I am confident that I made the correct decision to continue working with Oscar and Mary. Perhaps my future will progress in the pawnshop business." He is so deep in thought that he falls off to sleep for several hours.

As he is deep in slumber, his mind wanders back to his younger years, where he vividly recalls working at his grandfather's Bar and grill and cherishing the moments spent living with his parents in the old adobe casa.

However, regardless of the situation, his soul was consistently urging him to depart, and now he knows the real reason. With the newfound knowledge and a deeper comprehension of faith's intentions, he can now take a moment to reflect on the incredible journey he has embarked upon.

Antonio wonders why he was chosen by a higher power, connected with Luna, for a particular purpose. Asking himself does his life have a greater meaning than what meets the eye. Has he been the chosen one? Would it be wise for him to place trust in the concept of divine election? Did God or Luna grant him this special power?

As the wind whispers in his ears, he begins to feel a sense of power within, a hidden reservoir of untapped energy. He now has trust in his abilities. Appreciative he can speak with the spirit, Luna, be advised by the whispers of the wind, and develop a deep-rooted belief in himself. A core he has never experienced before.

Thinking, "Am I transcending the ability to have the foresight over faith itself? I am developing the power to see into the future and the past."

When Antonio wakes up the following morning, he is overcome with a newfound sense of confidence and authority that he has never experienced before. Standing tall at the helm, he embraces his role as a leader, steering the ship with determination and guiding it towards its destination. His vision, far from being a mere dream, exerts a powerful influence that drives him steadily towards his destined path. Yet, he is still unsure what it may be.

As he entered the kitchen and made his way to the breakfast table, he was delighted that Mary had already prepared a delicious meal of eggs and toast. With a smile on his face, he confidently took a seat and assumed control of the conversation. Saying,

"In the event that we secure a significant amount of funding for the candlestick antique holder, our plan is to embark on an ambitious project of expanding and remodeling the pawnshop. Our primary goal is to curate a captivating environment that appeals to both residents and travelers alike. The diverse assortment of products we offer, coupled with the enchanting stories that accompany each piece, will undoubtedly enthrall anyone who visits."

Both Oscar and Mary were equally impressed with Antonio's suggestion. Saying,

"Expand, not size down?"

Antonio expresses his desire for us to establish the most prominent and exceptional pawnshop in the city, one that will entice and captivate everyone to visit. Saying,

"Imagine the store as a radiant garden, a place where visitors flock drawn to a force that lies within. Calling others to come and wonder and find the undiscovered. As soon as our door swings open, the hearts of visitors are also opened, creating a warm and welcoming atmosphere upon their arrival. The construction of this event will undoubtedly attract a great number of individuals who will be eager to witness the magnificence of history, and it is our obligation to make it accessible to others."

Mary asks, "Are you sure Antonio?

He replies,
"The renovation costs will be taken care of using the gold coins in my possession, and the proceeds from the candlestick holder will create a collection of historical artifacts."

Arriving at the store after breakfast, both Antonio and Oscar start to plan the remodel and expansion of the shop. The store next door has been emptied for years after a shoe repair business closed. Oscar called his landlord, asked to see the interior, and he discussed his expansion plan. The landlord had reservations, however, not costing him any money and the fact that Oscar would invest in and remodel the vacant space, he gave them a minimum rental fee.

Oscar followed Antonio's new vision with gratification saying,

"Despite his long-standing desire to expand, he hesitated to take action on his own, particularly in light of Mary's waning enthusiasm for the business."

Antonio brings a new spark of light into both Oscar and Mary's hearts. A moment of profound magic, like a symphony played in the whispers of the wind. Picture a tale of wonder, where life bursts forth in a blaze rather than in silence, giving rise to a brand-new adventure in that very instant.

Tonight, Antonio is going to meet Luna and take the opportunity to share with her his new direction and future plans. Hoping to receive her blessing and approval, he wanted to express his gratitude towards her for guiding him towards the right path in life. Encouraging him to embrace reality instead of holding on to a childhood fantasy was essential in his growth.

The day was filled with extensive discussions and meticulous planning before they decided to wrap up and go home for the evening. Antonio is experiencing a whirlwind of thoughts as he ponders the questions he wants to pose to Luna.

Upon stepping into their home, Antonio was greeted by the sight of a letter addressed to them from Mexico, which had been carefully placed on the kitchen table. The reply that he had been eagerly waiting for, from his mom, however, contained a sorrowful message.

The mother wrote a letter expressing that his father had passed away due to an infection in his body the week before. Despite taking the prescribed medication and using the leaf from the Tree of Life, there was no improvement in his condition.

Antonio put his head down, holding it in his hands, finger interweaving, and cried, as if his heart was torn out. His heart earlier was a vibrant tapestry of dreams and excitement and now a symphony of ache and sorrow. His grief, his burden, and his regrets caused his tears to fall like rain. Was it the gods or spirits that betrayed him? Why did this happen?

Despite his trembling hands and aching heart, he still managed to forge a thought to survive and prosper deep within his heart. Upon receiving the heartbreaking news, Oscar, and Mary immediately rushed to his side, tenderly holding his hand and enveloping him in a deep, comforting embrace. But that would not bring his father back.

As he entered his room and opened the window, he was immediately embraced by the soft, warm whispers of the breeze that surrounded him. As the wind gently blew, Antonio could hear his father's voice calling out to him, urging him to take care of his mother.

His thoughts drift back to his childhood, memories of family times, and love. As the only son, his thoughts are like the current in the river of life. As the seasons change so do the tides of our hearts. Antonino remembers his fathers, as steady as a lighthouse, a deep-rooted tree unwavering. Providing him with assistance and understanding as he navigates his emotions, passing no judgement. Acting as a guiding presence, helping him navigate through the various challenges and experiences of his childhood.

Even in moments when the stars feel far away, the love within a family remains unwavering and unconditional, surpassing all boundaries. The love that his father had for him will always stay deep within his heart. His soul was deeply wounded by the unpleasant news, leading to a predictable decision of not seeking Luna tonight.

In the late muted hours, as the warm breeze whispers in his ears, his bed once a sanctuary, now becomes a battleground. Unable to sleep, counting each breath, along with regrets. It was a night filled with various obstacles, making it nearly impossible to unwind and find a peaceful sleep.

As the sun poured through his bedroom window the next day, its radiant beams enveloped him, infusing his body with their powerful energy and lifting him to a heightened state of being. It was evident that his spirit and drive had returned, a new day to move forward.

CHAPTER 10

The start of Antonio's day brings a sense of imbalance as he awakens, his body feeling the effects of a restless night with only a few hours of sleep. Although he attempts to shrug off the negativity, the profound pain of loss lingers within his being.

Seated at the breakfast table, the atmosphere was somber, no words were spoken. The ticking of the clock on the wall became prominent. As Antonio, Oscar, and Mary, consumed their meal.

Like a lightning bolt striking the sound of a ringing phone sounds, Mary rises to answer. The phone I.D flashed Mr. King's name, as she placed the call on speaker, hearing,

"Mary, congratulations your candlestick holder has been authenticated, and we have an offer from a collator to purchase it. Would you like to hear the offer?"

Mary replies, "Yes of course?"

According to Mr. King, the collector is willing to pay a hefty sum of $25,000 for the antique. In the quiet chamber of anticipation, a spark of revelation follows. As all three individuals stood, their hearts were filled with excitement, and the room seemed to overflow with endless possibilities, as the good news burst forth like a magnificent exploding star.

During the phone conversation, an agreement was reached between the parties involved, with Mr. King making a commitment to send the sales contract and a check via overnight mail. The check will be for the agreed amount, minus the sales fee of $2,500, which Mr. King will deduct for his services.

Although Antonio's father's situation is unfortunate, the excitement of the call momentarily pushed it aside. It was a gloomy and rainy day when we arrived at the pawnshop, and to our disappointment, business was slow. When it rains in Tucson, most residents prefer to stay indoors and avoid going out.

Antonio, feeling bored and having nothing to do that afternoon, was too depressed to rummage through the back room of the shop. As a result, he decided to sit and watch TV until something caught his attention. Eventually, his eyes landed on a small wooden jewelry box, which was placed high on a storage shelf. Taking it off the shelf, he opens the box and is astonished to find that it begins playing a beautiful melody.

Wiping the dirt and dust out, he sees something inside of interest, a beautiful silver necklace with a blue pendant attached. The pendant is shaped like a star as it sparkles in the dim light. Placing it in the palm of his hand he examined it closely, finding etchings of small birds and strange animals on both sides. Is it possible that this jewelry piece could be an ancient artifact worn by a princess from a Native American tribe?

As he held it, the heat from his hands changed the colors of the stone from the color of blue skies to yellow sunrises in the east. It is intriguing to wonder what he has stumbled upon in the old storage facility situated in the back of the store. Antonio carefully placed the pendant in his pocket, intending to examine it later when he got home this evening.

Entering his bedroom, he placed the pendant on his dresser for examination later, but tonight he wants to visit Luna and seek her advice and guidance. As the sun is setting after dinner, he prepares for his walk to the park to discuss two events that are heavy in his heart and mind. One, his father, and two his realization of the newfound power and understanding he has developed.

As he slowly makes his way towards the local park, his eyes fixate on the towering giant saguaro cactus. As he takes each step forward, his anticipation builds up gradually, growing stronger and stronger, until he finally arrives at his destination. The spot we are referring to is located right before the base of the cactus, and it happens to be the exact destination where the portal doors inexplicably open up. Antonio finds solace in deep meditation, where he vividly imagines her captivating face and mesmerizing emerald eyes, eagerly awaiting her arrival.

Several hours later, in the darkness of the moonless night, the portal doors open and Luna appears, reaching for his hand. Stepping into the grand chamber, the heavy doors shut firmly behind him, leaving him in a state of weightlessness that he had never experienced. Picture yourself being embraced by a comforting sensation similar to being wrapped in cotton, while being effortlessly swept away by the wind, resembling a delicate dust ball.

The experience of traveling through time can be quite disorienting, as you do not know your destination. Experiencing the beauty of time can be a truly captivating and mesmerizing experience. Luna holds his hand firmly as they both float into space reliving past and present moments in a different world.

Luna does not speak as she flows through space and time, her long hair blowing behind her as an angel flying through space, pulling him along. Remembering time travel allows us to venture into the past, future, and present. It is an intriguing phenomenon.

Once their movements come to a halt, he gazes down to see an image of his father lying in bed, tightly clutching his mother's hand, both patiently waiting for the inevitable moment when his father will peacefully pass away. Luna speaks her first words, saying,

"Your father peacefully transitioned into a better world, a place where he can finally find eternal serenity. I wanted to show you his transition, sometimes the leaves from the tree of life, fail as we all do." Antonio, the nostalgia of revising cherished memories, alters your life and tugs at your heartstrings. I wanted you to visit this moment.

They stood side by side, their eyes fixed on the sight before them, as his father's soul gracefully ascended from the bed and embarked on its celestial journey into the heavens. Luna takes Antonio's hand, saying.

"How about we make our way back to the grand coliseum hall, find a comfortable spot to sit, and take the opportunity to delve into a conversation about your future and any uncertainties you may have."

Immediately upon their arrival, they promptly headed to the great hall, where they took their seats, fulfilling their original purpose.

Luna expresses to Antonio that,

"She has been diligently observing every step he has taken and every decision he has made, noting that all of them have been honorable. She expresses her pride in his ability to take control of his life and make important decisions independently, recognizing that each decision adds to his personal power and vitality. Your decisions will lead you to success and contentment. So, follow your heart, look how far you have come."

Luna walks him to the portal doors, as they stand before them the doors open leading Antonio to the park in front of the cactus. As he exits, Luna tells him,

"I will be watching out for you, Antonio. Continue your journey."

The portal doors close and the sequoia is back to normal, standing tall in the night.

Back at the house, Antonio retrieves the pendant from the top of the dresses, admiring its changing color, trying to figure it Origen. In previous times, was it a valuable commodity that could be traded for buffalo skins, food, or weapons? It is possible that this item could have served as a necklace for a queen or chief belonging to a native American Indian tribe.

Exhausted from his long journey with Luna, he succumbs to sleep, oblivious to the gentle whispers carried by the wind.

The following morning, he goes back to the store and retrieves the wooden box in which the pendant was discovered. With careful attention, he meticulously examines the lining and interior of the box, delicately pulling back a layer of red velvet to reveal a surprising discovery - a map on aged parchment paper, cleverly concealed within the folds of the lining. Filled with a combination of eager anticipation and a sense of curiosity, his mind begins to spin with excitement, eagerly looking forward to embarking on yet another adventure that will be guided by a newfound map.

The distance between Tucson and Zion National Park in Utah is quite significant, as one can observe when studying the route. Stretching all the way from the sun-kissed desert in Arizona, through the vast expanse of land, to the majestic red rock canyons of Zion National Park in Utah, which lies approximately five hundred miles to the north.

When he informed Oscar and Mary about his new quest, they immediately questioned how he would make the trip on his own. Without access to a car or driver's license, undertaking this trip becomes a laborious and demanding endeavor. But he is quick to respond, "A Bus."
Antonino heads to his room, opens his door, and with a quick glance at his backpack and a swift grab of some cash from his drawer, he promptly makes his way to the bus station in Tucson. Purchases a ticket from Tucson to St. George Utah just a short distance from Zion National Park, a quick decision.

With the sun gradually sinking in the Arizona sky, painting the cactus-studded landscape with elongated shadows, his grand adventure begins. Our road trip is driven by an insatiable curiosity and the excitement of uncovering hidden wonders. As he gazed out of the bus window, he was captivated by the sight of the majestic mountains that stood tall, reaching the heavens.

The bus glided along the hot asphalt road, its wheels producing a harmonious tune that echoed the melodies of the desert. As he embarked on the ride, he estimated it would take approximately twelve hours, including stops along the way. As he embarked on the journey, he could not help but be amazed by the awe-inspiring view of the painted desert, with its vibrant colors and majestic landscapes. Furthermore, he took notice of the fact that the barren wasteland, despite its desolate appearance, was surprisingly embellished with occasional bushes and cacti, serving as a minor source of life within the otherwise barren landscape. The view before him stunningly combined sheer beauty and heavenly tranquility, leaving him in awe and peace, as he fell asleep in his seat while watching the sand grains sparkling in the distance.

Arriving at the bus station in St. George, Utah, it was just a short distance to Zion Park perhaps ten miles. Antonino feels the urge to stretch his legs after being seated on the bus for a long period, prompting him to choose to walk as the means to reach his destination.

Seeing the breathtaking view before him revealed Bryce Canyon, where stones stood like ancient sentinels, their surfaces intricately carved by the unforgiving winds and the relentless march of time. As the sun was setting, hues of apricot and lavender colored the rocks. The sandstone cliffs soared like giant cathedrals.

Checking his map, it revealed a starting point at the Virgen River at a location called Angels Point. Deciding to camp out for the night he removes his sleeping bag from his backpack, placing it along the side of the Virgin River, hearing the sound of the river's song. Lying beneath a tree, he sees the magic of the Utah skies, with the Milky Way filling the sky, with all its Splendor.

As he prepared to settle down for the night, he took off his shoes, which were covered with the red dust from the soil. As the night grew muted, he could feel and hear the steady rhythm of his heartbeat, lulling him into a peaceful slumber. Instead of having a campfire tonight, he decided to rely on a few basic items from his pack to keep him company. With a soft murmur, the wind whispered in his ears, imparting the knowledge that his journey would begin the next day and that by faithfully following the map, he would find his path.

CHAPTER 10

As he wakes up at sunrise, he leisurely strolls towards the river, where he proceeds to splash the cold, invigorating water on his face. He then cups his hands and gathers several handfuls of the fresh, crisp water from the running spring river, drinking it down to quench his insatiable thirst.

Having made all the necessary preparations, he is now prepared to embark on an exciting adventure. Armed with an ancient map, its yellowed pages, and barely visible lines, he eagerly departs to a forgotten location and perhaps a lost treasure.

His fingertips gently followed the faint traces of ink that had weathered over time, mapping out the intricate lines on the aged parchment. On the parchment, there were no labels or symbols to be found. Instead, it simply displayed a starting point and a clear path following the Zion River, leading towards a peculiar marking that indicated twisted trees at the point where the river splits, this was his destination. He followed the path of the map, each step echoing anticipation.

When he arrived at the fork in the river, he noticed how the vines tightly clung to the moist rocks, creating a stunning sight. However, he soon realized that the map abruptly ended at this point, leaving him uncertain about the exact location of the hidden treasure he had been desperately searching for. Nevertheless, he remained hopeful that the treasure could be found somewhere in the vicinity.

Exploring the area, was he seeking a cave, a corridor leading into the mountain, or a burial location? As the sunset, still not knowing what he was seeking. He decided to camp at the splitting rivers, and lesson the whispers of the wind and images from the moonlight that evening.

His stomach growled with hunger as he picked the berries from the local bushes to consume. The moon is full, lighting the forest below, as he examined the map. As he scrutinized it more closely, he discovered a small drawing of a heart-shaped stone. Bathed in a soft glow, a heart-shaped carving caught Antonio's attention as he gazed at the red rock, which was directly illuminated by the moonlight, and was located across from him. Was this the clue he was searching for?

In the moonlight, he walked to the red granite stone and examined the heart shape etching. Removing his pocket knife he began to chip away at the stone, breaking off one piece at a time. With each passing moment, his digging grew increasingly persistent, until finally, a small hollow opening materialized.

By inserting his finger into the hole, he could detect a cloth-like material, which he then carefully extracted using his fingers. The cloth, which is rolled up neatly, is secured tightly with a decaying piece of twine. He removed the twine and untied it, revealing a cloth that contained yet another drawing of the landscape, specifically a local map of his exact location.

By now it was too dark to see his surroundings, he placed the map in his pocket and lay in his sleeping bag.

Despite his inability to sleep, he found himself in a state of vivid imagination, as he recalled a memory from his childhood - the image of his mother, tenderly placing a cold, wet cloth on his forehead when he was ill with a high fever. When he was too weak to eat, she lovingly fed him with a wooden spoon. The flashbacks continued to come one after another, relentlessly. Constantly, his thoughts were filled with his mom, never leaving his mind. In the future, it is imperative that he brings her to Tucson so that they can live together. His mind was entirely preoccupied with her well-being from that very night, making it impossible for him to focus on anything else. Could it be possible that the wind was trying to convey a message to him?

The night seemed to stretch on endlessly, and his excitement to explore with his recently discovered drawing kept him wide awake throughout the entire night, awaiting the sun to rise.

After what felt like an endless period, a minuscule fraction of sunlight appeared in the distance, as if from a different world. As the sun begins to rise, its rays gradually illuminate the treetops, casting a soft glow and unveiling the majestic silhouettes of mountains and fluffy white clouds.

As soon as he took the cloth map out of his pocket, he swiftly placed it on the sand, attempting to decipher its location. He located an X on the mountainside where the heart had been etched. Along the course of the river, characterized by double lines, a magnificent tree is portrayed in a striking illustration, standing alone and commanding attention. At the base of the tree, there is a clearly visible X that has been marked. Could it be possible that this is the exact location he has been searching for?

Over history, there have been numerous instances where valuable treasures have been discovered, while others have mysteriously disappeared, all of which can be traced back to the legends and enigmas of the past. Without a doubt, pursuing or discovering a treasure is an endeavor that transcends time, captivating our imaginations, whether it be as hidden gems or a mere piece of forgotten history.

The flame of imagination burns brightly within every one of us.

Antonio makes his way downriver to the large tree, with grand expectations, searching the grounds around the tree he finds nothing. As he gazes towards the south side of the tree, a look of shock washes over his face when he sees the name LUNA, intricately carved into the bark of the tree. How could it be, Luna, carved her name here for Antonio to find?

He is in disbelief, was this journey a way to show him how to deal with disappointment and frustration whether you face setbacks and negatives? Occasionally, it may be disappointing to discover that the treasure is not to be found there. However, it is important to harness the power of emotions in order to navigate through challenges and stay committed to your quest.

In addition, it is of utmost importance to keep in mind the fundamental motives that compelled you to embrace risks, as they possess the potential to serve as a wellspring of motivation, propelling your endeavors and granting you invaluable insights. It is perfectly normal to feel disappointed when facing rejection, as it can be an opportunity for personal growth and acquiring new insights.

Antonio thinks should I be angry, or just accept the fact I failed in my journey. You traveled a long way, across a vast distance, fouled by hope and determination. Your heart carried dreams, guided by whispers of forgotten promises. The map you unfolded was more than ink markings. When we finally found Luna's name, the journey ended, and we were disheartened to find no Seguro cacti nearby to offer our prayers for Luna's help.

With a heavy heart, he positioned himself at the bottom of the tree's sprawling trunk, cradling his head in his hands as a single tear of disappointment escaped his eyes.

With his stomach aching for food, he made his way back to the main road, stopping at the first fast food facility he discovered, a Mc Donalds. Seated comfortably at his table, he found himself unable to resist the temptation of indulging in whatever he desired, taking bite after bite, until his stomach was completely satisfied. At the moment, a hamburger never tasted so good.

Continuing his walk to St. George and locating the bus station, he purchases his ticket for the journey home to Tucson, Disappointed but puzzled why Luna had him undertake this journey.

When he arrived home the following morning, he made sure to tell both Oscar and Mary about his unsuccessful quest. Then heads to bed for some well-deserved rest. The gentle warmth of the breeze flowing through his window fills his ears, as his mind drifts towards the anticipation of visiting Luna later in the evening.

Upon awakening to the sound of Mary cooking in the kitchen, he slowly rises from his bed with a noticeable expression of disappointment and unhappiness. He remained puzzled, wondering why he felt such intense emotions that compelled him to embark on this journey.

The table was filled with a sense of quietness that evening as everyone came together to empathize with Antonio and share in his grief.

CHAPTER 11

After dinner, Antonio set off to visit and sit in the park, arriving early he sat before the large Seguro, watching the sunset, skies turning from blue to deep red and black. Hours passed, and his focus on Luna's face and emerald eyes filled his mind.

Suddenly, there was a powerful monsoon lightning strike. The park was hit with rain as it came pouring down. The rain is falling from the heavens with a soothing purr, resembling the gentle waves of the ocean.

The cactus portal doors opened, and before him stood Luna, in all her beauty. Reaching for Antonio, asking him to follow her to the great hall, they walk together. Sitting with the golden veil separating them, Antonio asks,

"Luna, why did you send me on a journey, knowing I would fail?

Luna, replies,

"Antonio, disappointment is inevitable, it is part of our lives. We all handle it in different ways, it defines our resilience and growth. If you face a setback, it is a normal emotion."

Antonio asking,

"But why me, my life has been all positive and rewarding since I befriended you?"

Luna replies,

"Reflect on your expectation, sometimes we set the bar too high, are you being reasonable? Disappointments can be powerful lessons, use them as an opportunity to learn and grow. Focus on the one at hand, comforting your mother and bringing her here with you, and move forward. You will always experience unexpected storms, unravel the threads, and recalibrate your compass. I must leave now."

She firmly grasped his hand, guiding him confidently through the portal door and into the relentless rain and fierce winds. With a heavy heart and completely soaked by the rain, he walked home, not expecting the answer he received.

As he arrives home, he notices the household is fast asleep, and upon entering his room, he is greeted by the sound of raindrops pounding forcefully against the glass, resembling the rhythmic beating of a drum.

Not only did he experience disappointment in finding nothing on his trip to Zian Park, but he also received a negative reply from Luna, adding to his feelings of letdown. Despite the pouring rain, Antonio opened his window to listen to the sounds of the wind, hoping for some guidance.

His feeling of emptiness is a vague, unconformable feeling that was difficult for him to identify with. In his heart, he feels numbness, and detachment and has lost his sense of being, a feeling that defies description.

The nostalgia evoked by this feeling brings him right back to his childhood when he frequently found himself in a state of helplessness and isolation. The profound words of Luna continue to linger in his mind, serving as a constant reminder that the key to healing and finding fulfillment lies in acknowledging and understanding one's emotions.

With the rhythm of the rain, António falls off to sleep with his heart still filled with disappointment.

When the following morning arrived, he woke up to the warm embrace of bright sunlight, relieved to find that the rain had finally ceased and the ominous dark clouds had drifted away. The gentle rays of sunlight that flooded the room brought forth a surge of warmth that filled my heart and instilled a profound sense of existence. Today I feel a scene of being needed in the tapestry of human emotions. There is a thread that binds us all, and today I will find that connection.

As I walk into the kitchen and join Oscar and Mary, I cannot help but feel the comforting fabric of the community surrounding me. At that moment, the sense of loneliness dissipates, and I am filled with gratitude for the blessings I have, I am given a new day.

When I gaze around the table, where laughter gracefully dances and memories beautifully bloom, what I see is pure joy, a magical ambiance that fills the air. The gentle breeze carries the tantalizing scent of bacon, eggs, and a piping hot cup of coffee, creating an irresistible atmosphere. The promise of good things to come awakens my senses, filling me with anticipation. Antonio is back.

Oscar and I embarked on a journey to meet with the contractor, who had been entrusted with the task of remodeling the pawnshop. His name is Ted Thompson, a middle-aged man, who possesses an older pickup truck filled with basic tools and ladders for his work.

As we arrive at the store, Ted is leaning against the front door lighting a filterless cigarette and holding a paper cup of coffee. He was dressed casually, wearing jeans and a white tee shirt, with a tool belt hung at his side, he is a man who is ready to work. Oscar opens the doors, Ted assessed the surroundings and planned where to start. He requested that I remove the items from the area where he will be taking down a wall to join the two stores together.

Initially, my immediate thought was that I would have to invest my time in cleaning the entire inventory once more. However, looking on the bright side, this will provide me with an opportunity to thoroughly examine all the valuable antiques once again.

Oscar puts up a large sign on the front window saying, "Closed for renovations."

While enjoying a moment of peace and mute this morning, he opted to contact Pedro, the kind-hearted Coyote who had played a crucial role in his journey to the United States. To his surprise, he discovered he had kept Pedro's phone number safely tucked away in his wallet. Upon making the call, he told Pedro of his desire to have him bring his mother to Tucson. Pedro reminded him his travel was to just cross the Rio Grande river to America.

However, Antonio, offered a gold coin worth $ 2,000 to bring his mom further north of the river, and they agreed on the border town of Nogales in southern Arizona. Pedro will go visit Antonio's mom and discuss with her the arrangement for travel.

On the following day, Antonio was contacted by Pedro who shared that his mother had a preference to remain at home and be with her family, saying,

"Oaxaca, Mexico is where she was born, and it is also where she will spend her entire life until her death."

Once again, he finds himself in the midst of conflicting emotions, torn between the strong desire to be close to his mother and the unfortunate inability to visit or see her. He is feeling overwhelmed by the numerous choices that are being introduced into his life.

Antonio made the tough decision to separate from his family in order to pursue a more fulfilling and prosperous life, with the goal of eventually bringing his loved ones along on his journey to success. Deciding to leave was an incredible choice for him to make, but ultimately, he decided to follow his own path. Considering that he has reached the age of eighteen, which is commonly regarded as the age of adulthood, he can make his own decisions.

Luna's guidance will be crucial for him to stay on the right path, so tonight he will seek her counseling.

At the dinner table, both Oscar and Mary directed their attention towards him, asking about the source of his discomfort, which resulted in a visible expression of discontentment spreading across his face. He informs them of his mother's decision to stay in Mexico, despite his hopes of bringing her to America. The atmosphere in the room was heavy with disappointment, and his heart mirrored this sentiment, burdened by shattered hopes and unfulfilled wishes.

After finishing his meal and helping with the dishes, he informed them that he planned to take a stroll in the park to clear his mind and come to terms with his mother's decision. Upon arriving at the giant saguaro cactus, he took a seat in front of it, focusing his attention and calling upon Luna once again. This time, her arrival was swift, with no long wait.

As the Cactus portal doors swing open, Antonio makes his way inside and follows Luna into her chamber. Luna investigates his eyes and inquires what is disturbing him as his heart looks heavy and sad.

Antonio, tells her of his mother's decision and his disappointment.

Luna, says,

"Spirits guide you and are an integral part of your belief system. Spirits provide guidance, support, and wisdom to those who seek it. But they do not provide the answers to the journey of life. I am your spirit and will help guide you, but I cannot help you in making your life's decisions."

Continuing,

"There will be a day soon when the desire to separate from one's spirit will occur. It is a profound and complex experience, questioning your innermost essence, seeking answers, and letting go of your connection. Soon that day will come Antonio, questioning the need to reclaim your individuality. Separating from the spirit is paradoxical and ultimately leads us back to wholeness, and we find balance and newfound wisdom within ourselves."

Antonino, I apologize for the suddenness of my departure. I urge you to contemplate the subject we have just touched upon. Luna takes my hand and leads me through the portal doors out to the park.

After the portal doors have shut, the Seguro reverts back to its regular condition, standing tall in the night sky. A portal awaits, hidden in plain sight, not gold or silver but to enter and step beyond the mundane, to believe in the extraordinary. I have learned to experience this sensation at various times.

On my walk home, I hear the winds carrying secret whispers across time, it dances through the leaves and bends the branches of trees. Tonight, the park winds carried the scent of desert air and the scent of blossoms in the spring. It whispers tales of places afar where mountains rise from the deserts to the heavens. Over time, the wind can alter the shape of everything it encounters. The sensation is so powerful that it tingles through my entire body, causing me to feel overwhelmed with excitement.

Walking home this evening can only be described as an extraordinary, out-of-body experience, where I embarked on a mesmerizing journey that transcended the physical realm and offered a glimpse into a fascinating phenomenon that defied our usual perception of reality. It appears as though my consciousness is disconnecting itself from my physical form. Close your eyes and imagine yourself floating above your physical body, observing it from a distance as if you were an outsider.

I am now feeling the life-changing events of uncharted water, the moments, and memories, the twists and turns of life. Lately, all events feel monumental, taking me out of my comfort zone, I must learn to adjust and grow.

CHAPTER 12

Making changes can be a frightening experience, but tonight I have opened my window and will listen closely to the whispers of the wind, hoping to hear words of guidance, and understanding.

As I lie in my comfortable bed, my gaze is fixed upon the plain white ceiling above me, and my attention is drawn to the scattered yellowing water stains that mar the surface of the cracking paint. Once a smooth and white surface and now an aged, yellowing plane, with numerous cracks. Is this what life does to us over time?

Despite being only eighteen, I have acquired a wealth of knowledge and experience over the past two years, all thanks to Luna. As I close my eyes, I take a moment to reflect on all the incredible and unforgettable journeys we have embarked on together and the invaluable wisdom that I have absorbed along the way. The wind speaks to me in hushed tones, its whispers carrying valuable advice. I attentively absorb its guidance, feeling the soothing breeze enter my ears and travel through my mind.

The heaviness in my eyes intensifies, causing them to gradually close as I succumb to the inevitable pull of sleep. As I surrender to its embrace, a flurry of nostalgic images from the past begin to float and weave their way through the corridors of my mind.

When the following morning arrives, I wake up with a clear purpose in mind, which is to assist Oscar in renovating the pawnshop. Mary and I are sitting at the kitchen table when she informs me that Oscar left early to meet with Ted in order to start work immediately at the store. In a rush, I gulp down a dish of cereal and then promptly leave for the store.

As soon as I step foot inside and make my way through the entrance, an unusual sensation washes over me, creating a profound sense of disturbance. As I look around, I notice Ted diligently working on a ladder, carefully removing a wall in order to create a passageway. Meanwhile, Oscar is busy collecting the remnants of broken trash and placing them into a designated trash bin.

Oscar calls to me,

"Antonio come help remove the remnants and place them in the trash, my back hurts."

As I place the trash into a wheel barrel, and deliver it to the trash bin next to the rear door, I see something unusual. Reaching for the item, I find it is a bone of some sort. It is quite perplexing to discover a bone that bears a striking resemblance to a human thigh, inexplicably located between the walls of the store. I remove it from the trash and bring it to show Oscar and Ted.

Ted saying,

"It appears that we have stumbled upon a thigh bone from a skeleton, but it is quite baffling as to how it managed to end up lodged between the walls."

Oscar carefully places the bone on the top of the glass showcase, ensuring its secure positioning, and then he and his team proceed to demolish the remaining part of the wall. More skeleton bones have been found by Ted during his exploration. Throughout the meticulous process of removing each piece of bone, we have uncovered various body parts, including ribs, arms, and legs; however, the skull remains elusive.

Ted, suggest we call the police right away. Saying,

"Someone was killed and hidden between walls during the construction of this adobe building a century ago."

We all agree, to call the police and report our findings, and we all sit in wonderment. I lift the thigh bone from the counter and place it on my lap, close my eyes, and start to feel the vibrations of the era.

I feel the sun greeting me, casting shadows across the adobe walls of the Tucson store. The area is dusty, sand and wind blowing. The clatter of horses drawing carriages and the distant sound of the Southern Pacific railroad fill the air.

The city pulses with the life of cowboys and miners, and the new University sets the ambiance. The university on old Main Street stands tall with numerous students.

Charles Lindbergh visited Tucson last week, flying his Spirit of St. Louis echoing in the sky. Resident wondering what it would be like to soar above the saguaro cactus touching the heavens. But who was the bone from, a native American, or an old cowboy, but the question remains, why is it hidden between the walls?

Approximately thirty minutes later, the sound of a siren and flashing blue, and red lights fill the air. With its sirens blaring, a police car arrives and parks in front of the pawnshop. Officers Lenon and Swift, two individuals who work in different departments, both arrive at the store and proceed to enter it together.

We show them the findings, and it is at this moment that we all share the same sense of bewilderment. The corner is summoned to come and collect the findings, while a dedicated team diligently searches the walls and building for any clues that may shed light on the past.

Intending to continue my examination, I covertly stashed the thigh bone beneath my jacket, aspiring to transport it back to my room for further study. After a long day of watching the police, they took all the samples needed and returned to their police station. Very little remodel was accomplished that day At dinner, we updated Mary on the events that had occurred. Oscar reveals he is shaken and uncomfortable about the discovery in the wall. Saying,

"It's truly astonishing to think that I've spent forty years working in the shop without ever realizing that there was a body hidden in the wall behind me."

Completing my meal, I made my way back to the privacy of my room. After entering the room, I made sure to take a moment to close the door behind me, ensuring that I would have uninterrupted solitude. Using precise and delicate movements, I carefully extracted the thigh bone and proceeded to cleanse it meticulously in the sink, leaving no residue behind.

In order to ensure the process was fully completed, I carefully and gently dried it using a soft bath towel, effectively preparing it for its upcoming use. I went over to my bed, took a seat, and then proceeded to open the window before placing the bone on my lap. I hope that the whispers of the wind will provide me with additional information about this person I am trying to learn more about.

There must be a significant reason it was hidden in the wall. Who was it, who killed the individual, and why?

Closing my eyes and meditating, I remembered the lesson Luna told me about being more reliant on my own abilities. Telling me soon the day will come when you will need to reclaim your individuality and separate from your spirit. Therefore, tonight I will depend on the whispers of the winds and my own powers. Is this something I will be able to do?

In my dimly lit room, the breeze blows softly and the crackle of anticipation grew. Before me appeared a spirit, speaking to me in the silence of my room. Hair and eyebrows wild, and eyes that held the secrets of the past. He explains he was sent by Luna, his name is Apolo, and he is to guide me to the portals of the past, to unveil the enigma of the dead, and reach across time and touch the echoes of the soul. My heart is pounding with anticipation, another spirit in my life to explore.

I see my image step through the portal while my physical body remains on the bed. The landscape changed, dark sand and dirt as far as one can see. Bones and skeletons everywhere, the smell of death filled the air. Are we in a different world? The skies are a bright red, and vacant. I hear the echoes of lost souls as we enter a vast emptiness, nothing is in focus. Then before me, I see a figure, an old man, dressed in cowboy boots, hat, and jeans. Emptiness in his dead eyes, and he speaks in a soft deep tone. Saying,

"You found the remains of my body after almost a hundred years. I have been wondering when I would be missed, I'm Luke."

Continuing.

"Back in the day, kid, the old pawnshop held the role of a Wells Fargo stage station, a century ago. I remember two notorious horsemen stopping in to feed and water their horses, knowing a stage would be coming in soon. One pulled out his gun and shot me dead, and stuffed me in a vacant closet. That is all I remember."

Apolo, says,

"Sometime when they shut down the Wells Fargo station and converted the location to several stores someone must have found your body and placed it between the walls."

Luke says,

"Go away and let me be."

As Apolo guides me back to my bedroom through the portal doors, I am immediately greeted by the sight of myself sitting on the bed, fixated on the thigh bone.

Apolo bids me farewell and his spirit dissipates in the distance. I am left wondering if what just happened was my imagination or a real journey

The following morning returning to the pawnshop I take the bone with me, and place it behind the counter out of sight. Later that day as Oscar and Ted were working, the police came back to the store telling us they did not know, who the bones belonged to and the store's location was in the past Wells Fargo station.

The following day, the story of the bones discovered in the pawnshop was featured in The Arizona Daily Star, the local newspaper. Despite the ongoing remodeling of the store, numerous visitors, and customers flocked in by the dozens not only on that day but also in the subsequent days. Business was booming.

The shop became so busy that Mary decided to come back to work and help. Ted had finished the pass through and we spent our days putting back the collectable and cleaning the inventory.

During that evening, I sat at my desk and wrote Mom a letter telling her of my condition and the discovery Oscar and I made, and again asking if she wanted to come to Tucson.

CHAPTER 13

During the next several months, Oscar taught me how to test for genuine gold, silver, and about collectable coin and antiques items, His mind is full of a great deal of knowledge after all his years of experience. He and his magnifying loop can spot almost every imperfection on objects.

As several weeks went by without receiving a letter back from mom, the gentle whispering breeze seemed to suggest that it was time for me to go and visit her. I have not seen her in two and a half years, which is a long time. Knowing the potential danger of being caught while crossing the border, I informed both Oscar and Mary of my intention. Being an illegal immigrant has its potential liabilities. One of the worst for me was not being able to obtain a driver's license with proper identification.

I knew in my heart it was the right decision, and I am determent to make the trip. The plan was for Oscar to drive me down to the border town of Nogales, leave me there, and I would find a way into Mexico by crossing the river or receiving a ride. Leaving them both was challenging, we have become family. That evening, I filled my backpack with items needed, ready for my journey tomorrow morning, including several gold coins and five hundred dollars cash.

Early morning, Oscar and I leave on our two hours' drive to Nogales, he will be dropping me off at a truck stop just north of the border crossing. Inquiring with numerous drivers, I found one who would let me sit in the truck's trailer cargo area for two hundred dollars.

The truck is a milk refrigeration transporter, the refrigerator trailer was at least fifty feet long. The thirty degrees temperature would just be for some thirty minutes, I remove my jacket and bundled up before entering the trailer. I felt the truck starting to move, several minutes later it stopped at what I thought was the border crossing, and then we proceeded to move on. After a short distance, the truck stopped, I see the doors open we were in Mexico at a service station. The driver yelled,

"OK kid, get out."

Now to find a bus station. Purchase a ticket for the ten-hour ride to Oaxaca, Mexico. Just several buildings away was the ADQ Buss service, my ticket purchased, and I am on my way. Sitting next to the window. Exploring the Oaxacan coast from the road, I encountered breathtaking landscapes and small charming towns.

With my head pressed against the cool glass of the window, the soothing rhythm of the tires creates a drowsy effect, making me drift off to sleep. As I contemplate how I can surprise mom, my eyes naturally begin to close. Dreaming of my childhood, the horse farm and sitting at the table with mom and dad, all visions of the past.

Awaking when the bus stops in Oaxaca, the passenger de-board. I am home at last. Oaxaca boast a significant coastline to the south, along the pacific ocean. During the fifteen centuries the Aztecs occupied the city later it was conquered by the Spanish. Oaxaca is a land of ancient ruins with a vibrant culture in the city. The desert is drench with glaring sun.

The ranch mom and dad lived on and worked is twenty miles inland from the ocean and mostly flat land and green meadows. From the bus stop at Oaxaca, I walked the five miles to the ranch. Having grown up here, I knew most of the surrounding area. With every step I take towards our old home, the memories become more vivid and overwhelming.

As the sun dipped below the horizon, each step brought me close to the old adobe. Thinking this visit will certainly surprise mom. The closer I become to the house, the more my heart fluttered with anticipation. The winding road is ending, as I approach the front door.

Knocking twice, the door opens, and mom is standing before me wearing a blue housecoat and her hare tied back in a ponytail.

I say,

"Surprise Mom."

Frozen in fear, she remains motionless, resembling a statue. Despite being a bit older and having some graying hair, her eyes still sparkle with youthful vitality. Her arms open, and hugs me tightly, asking,

"Why are you here?"

Clinging tightly, she weeps, allowing tears to run down her face. Stepping inside, I make my way to the table and take a seat, instantly engulfed in the intoxicating scent of cinnamon rolls permeating the room. My attention is immediately drawn to the necklace and heart she always wears, as they were given to her by my father.

Sharing the story of my journey to her, I made it a point to convey the overwhelming emotions that were stirring inside me, yearning for her presence. With each word that left my lips, her eyes became filled with tears that eventually streamed down her face. As we sit at the table for hours, I enthusiastically share with her the countless adventures, travels, and experiences from my work.

The exchange we had was filled with emotion, as she shared with me the difficult stories of the past few years since my father's passing, which have taken a toll on her. She shared with me the challenging decision she made to forgo coming to Tucson and instead remain in a familiar and comfortable environment. I realized she had faced various hardships and I could feel the weight of those experiences.

After a dinner of corn, chili, and beans as the sun starts to set, I decide to take her on a walk and tell her of Luna, my guiding spirit. In fact, I made the deliberate decision to take her to the same location where I initially found Luna, which is near the breathtaking saguaro cactus and the exquisitely pristine pond. The location itself holds a special significance as it was where I first encountered Luna, the girl with a stunningly beautiful face and mesmerizing emerald eyes.

After enjoying a delicious dinner in the late afternoon, my mom and I slip on our sandals and venture out into the desert's warm embrace for a leisurely walk. With every stride, our feet sank deeper into the dry desert sand, creating imprints that marked our journey through the arid terrain.

While I make my way forward, I find myself irresistibly drawn to the awe-inspiring panorama of the immense saguaro, its graceful limbs enveloping the peaceful pond in a tender embrace. As I walk towards the familiar Saguaro, the one that initially introduced Luna to me, a wave of nostalgia washes over me. While leading mom by her hand, we carefully navigated through the prickly embrace of the cacti.

In the remoteness, I see the waves of heat rising and dancing on the horizon. As we approach the oasis, we sit and look out over the pond, hearing the song of the coyotes.

Mom, asked,

"Why did you bring me here?"

I tell her,

"It is my desire for you to meet Luna, the spirit that has been faithfully guiding and protecting me over several years."

When I speak of Luna, my mom gazes at me with a bewildered expression, as if she thinks I am completely out of my mind and cannot comprehend what I am saying.

I instructed her to sit beside me and asked her to focus on a stunningly beautiful girl who emerged from the crystal-clear pond, her eyes sparkling like emeralds. For the moment, mom sits and does what I say.

The Mexican landscape is parch, the skies are anticipating rain, The clouds are full with moisture, the heavens can no longer hold the rain, and the skies open, emptying its lifeblood on the desert. Mom sits beside me, dripping wet and patronizing my request.

Suddenly we hear thunder, the primal roar of the heavens, lightning strikes and flashes across the skies, then all becomes silent.

Upon turning my attention to the pond, I am greeted by the sight of Luna's head and hair becoming visible. Her Emerald eye glowing, mom grabs my arm tight, as if seeing a ghost for the first time. I place my arm around her shoulder comforting her, and tell her,

"This is Luna, my guarding spirit."

Each of their eyes became intense as they locked onto the others, filling the air with a crackling tension, or perhaps it was a recognition. Luna, having just come from the pond, locked eyes with my mom, as if they shared a sense of familiarity.

Without a word being said. Luna extended both of her arms towards us, beckoning for both mom and me to follow her as she guided us towards the towering giant saguaro cactus. As we neared the entrance, the majestic portal doors gracefully swung open, beckoning us forward, and under Luna's guidance, we were ushered into the enchanting inner chamber. In a state of shock and astonishment, Mom joined us on this unexpected journey. The moment we stepped into the grand coliseum, my mom's expression turned to one of disbelief, questioning how it was possible for a Seguro with a circumference of just five feet could accommodate such an enormous space. I let her know we are venturing into a different realm of time and space, a realm where Luna both exists and traverses.

Luna, says to mom,

"I will take you both to the future, so you can see what life holds for you. Antonio's wife, children, and your role as a grandmother." As we hold hands, a sense of timelessness envelops us, transporting us through the vast expanse of time and space.

With the elusive sensation of time travel either to the past of future you pass through vast corridors, as the air crackles.

Eventually, we arrive at a place that feels oddly familiar, reminiscent of Oscar and Mary's charming home in Tucson, upon taking a second look, it is. Looking below, I see an image of me, must be twenty-five of more.

I am sitting on the sofa, which was previously owned by Oscar and Mary, while holding two small boys who are approximately two years old. With a plate of cookies in her hands, my mother is right by my side, eagerly handing them out, each treat adorned with vibrant rainbow sprinkles. Tony, who was sitting on my knee, reached out his arms and called for his mom.

It was a magical moment when Rosa, the woman who I will someday meet and marry, gracefully entered the room.

Luna, says,

"In the future, there may come a time when you will travel to America, where you can reside with your son and his wife, assuming the responsibility of caring for your grandchildren, all while Antonio and Rosa dedicate their time and efforts towards their flourishing business."

I ask Luna,

"She informed me that Oscar and Mary, after you got married, crossed over the rainbow, leaving you with both the house and business. Knowing that they are in a better place brings solace, and it is heartwarming to realize that they could bring happiness and improve your life."

After returning to the saguaro through the incredible power of time travel, Luna takes on the role of our leader. With her guidance, we pass through the portal doors, and she takes a moment to ask mom.

"Take a moment to imagine your life in the future. Do you see yourself happily surrounded by your son, daughter-in-law, and grandkids? Or do you prefer the solitude of your adobe on the farm?

Mom, speaks softly saying,

"With my son."

Once Luna departs, my mom and I begin the walk back to her home, both lost in deep contemplation about what lies ahead for us. In her own unique way, Luna could effectively guide her mom towards the right path for her future.

As we continue walking together, my mom starts saying,

"It is hard for me to comprehend what just occurred."

With Luna by my side, providing spritsail guidance, I assure mom, that we will always take the right path.

CHAPTER 14

Following hours of intense discussion, it is ultimately decided by mom that she does not wish to be alone, and instead, she chooses to pursue the vision of the future she has just encountered. It brings me joy to see that this is the choice that has been selected, as it aligns perfectly with my desires.

Telling mom, I will stay a few days and help her organize for the relocation and contact my coyote friend, Carlos to make travel arrangements.

It is truly astounding to see how minimal her possessions were during her time here on Earth. The adobe cottage, which belonged to the horse ranch, served as part of my parents' wages. She only has a small collection of dresses and jewelry, which comprises a few items that my father gave to her as tokens.

When I was a child, I never had the awareness of how little our family possessed, and therefore, I never experienced the feeling of being poor. But we were.

Tomorrow, my plan is to go to town where I will find Carlos and have a discussion with him regarding his guidance on how mom and I can successfully return to America.

While the evening progressed, mom engaged in a thoughtful process of selecting the ideal item to place in her backpack., one with memories and photos with loved one. She would leave a lot behind, but most were dishes, and cooking supplies easy to replace.

I called Mary and told her of my plan, and that mom was coming with me. She was eager to help her make a new life and befriend her. Mom could have my room and I would use the sofa until a solution was found.

The next morning, while I made my way into town to search for Carlos, memories flooded my mind with every tree, bush, and field I encountered. I must have climbed every tree I passed.

As I approached Oaxaca, I noticed that the gathering of residents had grown significantly, so I decided to walk with my hat on and head down in order to avoid being recognized. As I arrived at Toro's bar, which is a favorite hangout spot for Carlos, I took a seat at one table outside, eagerly anticipating his customary arrival. Without fail, he is always a devoted customer and makes sure to never miss out on a satisfying lunch.

As the clock struck noon and the sun reached its zenith, Carlos made his way up the dusty street, his footsteps echoing through the air, just as consistent as the familiar crowing of a rooster at daybreak. Entering Toro's, I call his name, he looks over and recognizes me, comes to sit at my table asking,

"Antonio, what are you doing back here?"

I let him know that my main purpose for coming was to find my mom, and I requested his aid in returning and crossing the river. Carlos is always helpful, especially if you will pay the right price. Upon showing him the two gold coins, he smiles back at me and inquired,

"Do you prefer going tonight or tomorrow?"

I tell him tomorrow, and he can leave me on the U.S. side of the river where I will arrange for Oscar to pick mom and I up. He stands, tells me it is time for his lunch, tips his hat and says before he walks away,

"Tomorrow here at 7:00 pm."

While drinking a cold ice tea, I call Oscar and tell in of my travel plan. Asking him to meet mom and I around 2:00A.M at a location just several miles from the border called Love's Travel stop. I instruct Oscar to carefully line the trunk with soft pillows so that mom and I can remain concealed inside until we reach our destination in Tucson. Now that the arrangements have been made, I can finally make my way back to the horse ranch, for our last night.

Mon is experiencing a bout of nervousness and is having doubts about going.

As the following day approached and our last hours at the adobe drew near, my mom continued to have doubts about leaving. We need to be concerned about the possibility of both of us getting caught, because if that happens, we won't be heading to Tucson, but to prison instead.

The time is getting closer to 5:00 pm as the late afternoon approaches. It is time for us to make our way to town as we have a gathering planned with Carlos. Because my mom's backpack is heavy, we decided to switch packs so that she could carry the lighter one, which was mine.

Arriving at Toro's bar, mom and I step in the back of the pickup truck, and slide under the blankets. Carlos starts his drive over bumpy dirt roads to a location secluded miles from town near the border and river. Once we remove the blankets, what lies before us is an expansive, open desert with nothing but sand and cacti visible for miles around. Carlos yells,

"Come on, lets go."

Ready to start our journey, Carlos holds out his hand, saying.

"Antonio, you have something for me, my friend?"

I remove the two gold coins from my pocket and place them in his palm, He says.

"Let's go."

Moving in a single file, we carefully tread through the thick brush and Thorney cactus, feeling the soft, warm sand beneath our sinking feet. With utmost caution, we skillfully maneuvered, ensuring we will not be noticed by the ever-vigilant border patrol

As the clock ticks for an hour, we finally arrive at the breathtaking Rio Grand River, where we are greeted by the mesmerizing sight of the setting sun. In the desert, the air is pristine and filled with purity, while a breathtaking array of colors illuminates the surroundings with vividness.

Carlos checks the skies for helicopters, and through his binoculars, surveys the surrounding. And says,

"Your destination, the United States is just across the river, stay well my friend. Mom holds on tight to my backpack as we walk across the slow-flowing river, the depth reaching the height of mom's nose.

Standing on the other side, I say ,

"Mom, we are in America."

The end of our thrilling adventure is just within reach as we navigate towards Love's Pit stop for the last stretch of our journey. Once we arrive there, Oscar will be joining us to celebrate the successful completion of our excursion driving us to Tucson   .

As I glance at my clock, I notice we are an hour ahead of our planned schedule, so it is currently 1:00 A.M. and my heart is again pounding with anticipation. My mom continues to stay silent and filled with fear. Nestled in the bush, we are situated just a stone's throw away from the station, allowing us to observe everything with a mere glimpse.

Despite being cold and wet, my mom continues to shiver without uttering a word, which is quite concerning. I take my jacket out of my backpack and kindly drape it around her shoulders in order to provide warmth and comfort.

As I gaze across the landscape, I am captivated by the subdued shades of brown and green. In the distance, my eyes catch sight of a jackrabbit, its ears alert and attentive to every sound. In complete silence, the two of us patiently wait, with my attention focused on Oscar's truck, anticipating its arrival at the gas pump. As my heart beats rhythmically, my anxiety intensifies with each passing moment. Finally, there is a sign of relief as the silhouette of Oscar's truck emerges from the distance.

As I look ahead, the sight of Oscar arriving at Loves Pit stop comes into view. As he proceeds to the pump to fill his gas tank, my mom and I quietly and stealthily approach the rear flatbed of the truck. We smoothly glide under the protective covering, signaling to Oscar that we are fully prepared to depart. He starts his motor and heads north to Tucson.

Mom finally begins to speak after being terrified during our journey, saying,

"I am struggling to comprehend the reason behind this task, as I was happy and at peace within the confines of my home."

Telling her to be patient the end of the journey is near, and she will be happy in her new environment, but I feel the bitterness growing. About an hour into our ride, Oscar pulls over and stops the truck, inviting us to come and set in the front. When he meets my mom for the first time, he greets her with a warm welcome and wraps his arms around her in a tight hug.

We move from the truck flat-bed to the interior with comfortable seats. In the distance, mom see the city of Tucson, with numerous buildings reaching toward the sky, a first for her. As we get closer to the city, my mom is in awe as she views the numerous populations that reside there. Upon arriving at the driveway, Mary cannot contain her excitement as she awaits the moment they will finally come face to face.

As I open the door, I extend my hand to help my mom step down onto the soil of Tucson. Standing beside me, she looks around at the countless homes and roads, as if she has been transported to a different world.

Mary asks mom? "What shall we call you?" Mom responds "Maria"

As soon as she stepped inside the house, mom was immediately enchanted by the comfortable coolness of the air conditioning, the sleek and modern design of the kitchen, and the tastefully decorated rooms. The transition from her humble adobe to a veritable house must have been overwhelming and full of excitement. When you see them side by side, it becomes apparent that there is a noticeable difference in their ages.

Mary gently takes her mom's hand and lovingly guides her down the hallway towards the small den, which she has transformed into a cozy bedroom just for her.

It is a small room with a window, a single bed, a dresser, and a closet. The room is enhanced by a brown and white area rug, which sits gracefully on the wood floor and adds a touch of warmth to the space. Mom and I will share the bathroom between our rooms.

Initially, the table setting that Oscar prepares is designed for two individuals, but as our family grows, it gradually expands to accommodate three and ultimately, it can even host four people. With her culinary skills, Mary has prepared a scrumptious dinner and now beckons us to join her at the table.

The table is beautifully set with a mouthwatering platter of zesty nachos, generously topped with seasoned ground beef, creamy refried beans, fresh green onions, juicy tomatoes, and savory olives, creating a culinary masterpiece that is truly fit for royalty.

Mom, begins to eat as the food is placed on her plate, and for the first time since we left a smile come over her face. As I gaze around the table, I cannot help but notice the expressions of contentment and glee on all four of our faces, and we are filled with gratitude for the opportunity to gather in this moment.

Mary raises her water glass, and says,
"I express my gratitude to God for blessing us with the presence of Antonio, his mother, and my husband, as they have played an instrumental role in creating a warm and loving atmosphere within our newly formed family."

The food at our house gets consumed quickly, and my mom says very little during the meal, mainly because she has a limited understanding of the English language. She instructs me to express gratitude to both Oscar and Mary for their warmth and hospitality, and I proceed to convey the translation.

With loving care, Mary guides mom to her room and provides assistance in helping her relax and unwind, recognizing the need for rest after a tiring and arduous trip.

With the culmination of a tiring journey, a full day of travel, and the consumption of a satisfying meal, the prospect of retiring to bed at sunset seems appealing.

As the night and the warm breeze fills the air, I lie and lesson to the whispers of the wind. My eyes close for a fleeting second and I become part of the vast expanse, a wonderer, a dreamer, and seeker of truth. As I gaze out of the window, observing the stars slowly emerging one by one in the night sky, I cannot help but feel a sense of awe and wonder. It is as if I am being drawn into a grand narrative, becoming a part of something much larger than myself.

The winds, with their whispered words and graceful movements, carry the secrets of my destiny, promising me thrilling adventures yet to be experienced. With its gentle softness surrounding me, I fall off to sleep.

CHAPTER 15

The next morning, as I wake up before everyone else, my first task is to make a fresh pot of coffee. I take my time sipping it, allowing the warm liquid to awaken my senses, and use this tranquil moment to reflect on the day that lies ahead. Shall I take mom to see the pawnshop, let her rest or unite with Mary at home?

Deciding on showing her the pawnshop, after her waking, eating and dressing, I walk with her to the store, passing through the park that contains the gigantic saguaro. As we approach the fearsome eight-arm monster, I turn to my mother and explain that this is the exact location where I meet Luna, my guiding spirit. As we make our way down the street, we continue until we finally reach the pawnshop. Once we enter the shop, we are warmly greeted by Oscar.

Mom's eyes open wide, and the sparkle of silver, bronze, and turquoise fill her vision. She has never seen so many antiques in her life. Spending several hours, she kept herself busy by thoroughly examining each object. She struggled to believe that I was a partner with Oscar in this business. Upon observing her, it has become clear to me where my curiosity stems from.

With grace and elegance, Oscar carefully selects a beautiful silver necklace from the shelf and delicately places it around my mother's neck. Saying,

"A special gift for a special person"

With a smile on her face, Mom nods her head up and down to acknowledge the gesture. Once we finished our lunch at Mc Donalds, I thought it would be a eventful idea to take my mom to the University History department in order to show her the items we donated, which were currently being showcased.

Since she lacked knowledge of U.S. history, she was unaware of the identity of General Custer and simply regarded him as a character depicted in a book and photo that was on display. We headed home mid afternoon for the day to spend time with Mary. When we walked into the kitchen, we discovered her sitting there with a Spanish translation book placed neatly on the table, as if she was determined to learn new words in order to better communicate with my mom.

As the days passed, mom found her place in the kitchen helping Mary prepare foods, cooking is an endeavor she enjoyed doing. After several days, I found mom becoming the housekeeper and cook, giving Mary more time to help at the pawnshop.

Every week, the number of customers coming to the shop has been increasing, resulting in a higher volume of item purchases and sales. As a result, the business is thriving. The pawnshop had become a source of inspiration and affection for Oscar and Mary, as they acquired a new insight into its value.

Additionally, I discovered a newfound motivation in my life that brought me immense satisfaction. By utilizing my knowledge and inserting the effort, I was not only building a future for myself but also providing a sense of security for my mom, Oscar, and Mary.

Mom is still feeling homesick, but I understand that adjusting to a new environment can take some time, it did for me.

The following morning, I awake to unusual weather here in Tucson, hazy skies because of overnight storms and dust blowing in the atmosphere. Considering the potential for a monsoon, we collectively agreed to close the store for the day and enjoy a cozy day at home.

The atmosphere is warm and cozy as we all sit together at the kitchen table, savoring our food and exchanging nostalgic tales. Oscar fondly reminisces about his childhood memories with his father in Mexico, where they would spend days surrounded by family, indulging in lavish meals and cherishing the company of cousins and loved ones. Both of his older sisters left home at the age of sixteen and were never heard from again.

Mary fondly reminisced about the days when she used to work alongside her mother, assisting her in cooking and selling food at their street stand located near the town.

My mom used to discuss how she would prepare meals for the horse ranch hands, making sure to serve them lunch and dinner, and always keeping food readily available for the help.

Through hard times, all the families remained unbroken, their bonds fortified by the land they called home. Their stories was a tapestry woven with threads of resilience, love, and the enduring beauty of the world around them. And as long as the winds blew and the sunset, their tale would continue, a never-ending story of a family's strength in the face of adversity.

Despite all the hardships they faced, they managed to survive by sticking together, filling their stomachs, and making the most of what little they had.

Despite their differences, the one common thread that bound them all together was the unwavering hope that someday, the circumstances would improve and they would find themselves in the exact place where they believed God intended them to be, in America.

All overcoming extreme obstacles along their journeys required resilience, adaptability, and a positive mindset, and above all stay motivated.

From listening to their stories, I acquired the understanding that each challenge we encounter in life is a chance for us to develop and acquire new knowledge.

Following the dinner that evening, I observed the rain outside, falling gracefully like slow drops from a cracked glass. My widow open lessoning to the wind carrying secret of gentle reminders and of journeys yet to be taken. It has been quite some time since I last saw Luna, and I am reminding myself that a visit is necessary.

While the others retire for the night, I take the opportunity to place my hat on my head to protect myself from the rain, as well as my jacket, before heading to the park. Exiting the door, I begin my leisurely stroll towards the majestic saguaro Cati, and once there, I find a cozy spot to sit and immerse myself in its peaceful atmosphere. Thinking of Luna, a cascade of memories fills my head. Once the rain finally ceases, my thoughts immediately become fixated on Luna, and I cannot suppress the urge to release a deep sigh. With each lightning flash, the subsequent thunder echoes through the air like an explosive boom, and in perfect synchrony, the portals of the cactus mysteriously open.

Before me stands Luna, her emerald eyes glowing with intensity, as she gracefully extends her hand towards me, guiding me towards the entrance of the inner chamber. I follow and sit across from her with the golden Vail between us. I sit in silence and lesson, as she says,

"Antonio, It has come time for you to follow your own spirit, and look upon the faces of those you have touched. You have now seen the spark of understanding and the flame of hope. All this has left a blessing and a promise within you, and you must proceed without my guidance. You have acquired the ability to see the future and past, visiting spirits, and leaving behind a legacy of knowledge by being in touch with life-forces."

I ask Luna,

"Why leave me now when all is going so well?"

She replies,

"Inevitably, there will be times when those we have provided guidance for, will feel a blend of disappointment and gratitude, but the influence from my guidance will leave an everlasting mark on your heart forever. You have the wind to help guide through your next journeys of life. Tonight, will be our moment of farewell, accept the transformation that comes with this ending, and know it comes with a new beginning."

In the silence that followed, the impression that I received is, I may never see Luna again. The emotion sinks deep within my soul, creating an emptiness and void as deep as the ocean.

Luna, rises, kisses my forehead, saying, "Antonio, it has been a gift to work and guide you, you will stay in my heart forever, as I will stay in yours. Remember, the powers given to me are now given to you, in your heart, to help and discover."

As I exit the portal doors, a torrent of tears cascades down my cheeks, resembling a ferocious thunderstorm. The weight of losing Luna, my guide, and mentor for the past two years, burdens me heavily.

Turning and watching the portal doors close, I am reminded of all the good that Luna had guided me through, now having a family, my mom, faith in myself, and the ability to help others. A strong accomplishment is significant, it showcases my ability to overcome a challenge, and to improve as life goes on. This approach will help in creating an interesting narrative in my life.

THE - END

Made in United States
Troutdale, OR
08/07/2024